She Startled Him And His Precarious Balance Was Shot To Hell.

Cooper flailed about, even as he spied a woman's rounded face and sparkling green eyes. Those eyes went from shining with amusement to widening in alarm as Cooper pitched forward, and fell on their owner.

His victim took the brunt of the fall, and became almost embedded in the moist soil. Cooper lifted his upper body from the woman's softly curved chest and leaned on his elbows.

L.J. breathed in deeply and stared upward into a pair of the bluest eyes she'd ever seen. She noticed that beyond giving her some breathing room, the man did not immediately budge. As a matter of fact, from the way he was ogling her, he didn't seem to have any intention of moving anytime soon.

Dear Reader,

A book from Joan Hohl is always a delight, so I'm thrilled that this month we have her latest MAN OF THE MONTH, *A Memorable Man*. Naturally, this story is chock-full of Joan's trademark sensuality *and* it's got some wonderful plot twists that are sure to please you!

Also this month, Cindy Gerard's latest in her NORTHERN LIGHTS BRIDES series, *A Bride for Crimson Falls*, and Beverly Barton's "Southern sizzle" is highlighted in *A Child of Her Own*. Anne Eames has the wonderful ability to combine sensuality and humor, and *A Marriage Made in Joeville* features this talent.

The Baby Blizzard by Caroline Cross is sure to melt your heart this month—it's an extraordinary love story with a hero and heroine you'll never forget! And the month is completed with a sexy romp by Diana Mars, *Matchmaking Mona*.

In months to come, look for spectacular Silhouette Desire books by Diana Palmer, Jennifer Greene, Lass Small and many other fantastic Desire stars! And I'm always here to listen to your thoughts and opinions about the books. You can write to me at the address below.

Enjoy! I wish you hours of happy reading!

Lucia Macro

Lucia Macro
Senior Editor

Please address questions and book requests to:
Silhouette Reader Service
U.S.: 3010 Walden Ave., P.O. Box 1325, Buffalo, NY 14269
Canadian: P.O. Box 609, Fort Erie, Ont. L2A 5X3

DIANA MARS
MATCHMAKING MONA

SILHOUETTE *Desire*®
Published by Silhouette Books
America's Publisher of Contemporary Romance

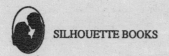

SILHOUETTE BOOKS

ISBN 0-373-76080-9

MATCHMAKING MONA

Books by Diana Mars

Silhouette Desire

Peril in Paradise #906
Mixed-Up Matrimony #942
Matchmaking Mona #1080

DIANA MARS

feels fortunate to be a part of the Golden Age of
Romance, which has seen so many exciting elements
added: suspense, horror, mystery, the supernatural.
Although she has worked in the fields of business, lan-
guages and anthropology, writing has proven to be the
strongest, yet most satisfying challenge.

One

Cooper Channahon winced as Mona stepped on his foot. Again.

The gangly fourteen-year-old absently apologized and went on her merry way, intent on reaching the dig and its director—her idol, Dr. L. J. Livingston.

Cooper took off his expensive Nike runners and rubbed the sore big toe. He was getting too old for this!

But fraternal love always proved his undoing. His younger brother Corbett, wandering around in a fog of child-rearing confusion and helplessness since his beloved wife Lauren had died, had needed some time to himself.

Mona, Corbett's only child, was a handful at any time, and since her mother's death, had thrown her considerable energy into her two passions: basketball and anthropology.

So Cooper had been enlisted to escort Mona to the excavation site after her varsity game. After a hellish day of stockbrokering, he'd almost forgotten his promise to Mona. When his niece had chastised him for not having proper attire for a dig, Cooper had just stopped off at an athletic shoe store. Mona had been slightly mollified when he'd let her choose two pairs from her other idol, Air Jordan: one for him, the other for herself.

But now his dear niece, totally insensitive toward his almost forty-year-old metatarsal, plowed ahead.

And plowed was definitely the operative word, Cooper reflected as his pristine Nikes lost their virgin state and became mired in mud. Swearing, Cooper replaced his crosstrainers, almost losing his balance, and got one foot out of the soggy field.

Only to have his other shoe become even further embedded in the sticky mud.

Cooper shook his head. What on earth had possessed him to accompany Mona to this unpleasant part of Illinois? Corbett's need for some private time to get his head together could have been served just as well if he'd taken Mona to a nice, safe mall, with a nice, clean multiplex.

As he made slow, painful progress toward Mona's

high-pitched, chattering voice, Cooper knew the answer.

He had never been able to say no to his two nieces. Of the three Channahons, Cooper was the only one who had never married. His baby sister Corliss was divorced, and the proud mother of adorable Maggie. Corbett, his widowed younger brother, was the loving if dazed father of mad, manic Mona...Cooper's own nickname for his niece.

But Mona didn't mind. She adored her uncle, and her uncle returned the affection tenfold.

Which was something Mona realized, and took advantage of on a regular basis.

So absorbed was Cooper in navigating the treacherous field without losing either his shoes or his balance, that he did not realize Mona had come back for him.

She startled him and his precarious balance was shot to hell. Cooper flailed about, even as he spied a woman's rounded face and sparkling green eyes. Those eyes went from shining with amusement to widening in alarm as Cooper pitched forward and fell on their owner.

Mona's squeals penetrated his cerebellum, but the woman he fell on did not even utter a sound as he slammed into her and drove both of them into the ground.

Even though he tried breaking his fall, Cooper

knew that his two-hundred pound frame would flatten anything in its downward arc.

His victim took the brunt of the fall and became almost embedded in the moist soil. Cooper lifted his upper body from the woman's softly curved chest, leaned on his elbows and said, "Dr. Livingston, I presume?"

L. J. Livingston breathed in deeply and stared upward into a pair of the bluest eyes she'd ever seen. She noticed that beyond giving her some breathing room, the man did not immediately budge. As a matter of fact, from the way he was ogling her, he didn't seem to have any intention of moving anytime soon.

Well, she'd certainly remedy that, L.J. told herself sternly.

"In the flesh," she said in her most professorial voice.

She groaned inwardly when she realized that her standard answer to the inevitable comments about her name took on a new meaning.

His blue eyes brightened and he seemed intent on continuing that line of thought when his legs straddled her thighs, and he seemed almost to be looking for a more comfortable position.

But he obviously recalled himself to his surroundings, which, at the moment, were mainly her. He got up in one fluid movement, then grabbed her hand and pulled her up with a mighty tug, freeing her from the mud encasing her backside.

But not before the clasping hook she had attached to the belt of her pants caught on his.

Some extraneous noise intruded into this pleasant predicament, and Cooper realized it was Mona, asking worriedly, "Are you guys all right? Or are you two in some sort of coma? You haven't answered me in aeons!"

Cooper did not bother answering, but L.J. did, calmly.

"Yes, we're okay. I may not have answered before because the wind was knocked out of me, but amazingly, I still seem to be in one piece."

Belatedly, Cooper looked over at the tall, handsome woman in front of him. Sheepishly, his eyes took in the formerly forest green blouse and slacks, as well as the smudges of mud on the woman's soft, pink cheeks. Her golden-brown hair was a mess, and it looked as if a family of pigeons had decided to make it its nest.

"I'm really sorry, Dr. Livingston. I'm sure your intention of studying this dig did not include scrutinizing it so intimately."

Although L.J. was sure the man did not mean anything by it, the word intimate seemed to float in the air between them, heavy with meaning and fraught with tension. L.J. knew the power of physical attraction on first sight, and after her disastrous experience in college with Nick, she zealously guarded against that type of experience.

Which was why she had to be especially careful with this man. Neither of them were teenagers, and the effect he was having on her hormones was magnified by age and experience.

"No, I can't say it did. I like getting into my work, but not this close up and personal." L.J. unclasped the hook bonding their belts and anatomy together, and stepping back a breathable distance, extended her hand. "I'm L. J. Livingston."

Cooper took the strong, long-fingered hand in his, and watched it being dwarfed by his own.

"Sorry about the mud," he apologized as their fingers made a sucking noise as they shook hands.

Mona giggled, and the innocent sound broke some of the tension between the two adults.

"No need to apologize, Mr.—"

"Channahon. But please call me Cooper." Blue eyes twinkling, Cooper added, "After all, I feel as if I really know you."

L.J. chuckled and said, "All right. And I'm L.J."

Looking at Mona, who was taking in the interchange between the two adults with avid eyes, L.J. added, "Your daughter is a delight. She's really enthusiastic about this project."

"Oh, he's not married," Mona added quickly. "Are *you*, Dr. Livingston?"

Taken aback, L.J. answered, "No, I'm not. Unless you happen to count my work," she added, smiling.

"I know what you mean," Cooper said, his eyes alighting on the soft, very kissable mouth.

L.J. felt his look like a gossamer touch, and caught herself before moistening her lips. Noticing the teenager's gaze shifting back and forth between her and her father, L.J. felt she'd better get herself together. Not only were teenage glands overactive and hyperactive at Mona's age, but teenagers seemed to think they had a vested right in interfering in everyone's business even while loudly proclaiming their God-given right to privacy.

"Oh? Are you interested in anthropology, too?" L.J. asked.

"No, I'm afraid that's Mona's department. She wants to be the next Margaret Mead or Dr. Leakey."

"Yeah. He says that anyone wasting their time on old bones and garbage doesn't have much of a life or any grip on the real world."

L.J.'s brown eyebrows shot up, even as Cooper's stomach plummeted.

"Oh?"

The single word was a death knell ringing loudly in Cooper's ears.

"I don't agree, but he thinks that anthropologists don't have a life. They just dig up someone else's past so they can live vicariously."

"I'd hate to think what—Cooper, was it?—thinks about librarians and other academics."

"Oh, they're just as bad, according to him. They

need to get their faces out of those moldy romances, and date some real men for a change.''

L.J. looked from Mona's big blue eyes to Cooper's, so similar to his daughter's, and said, "*I* read romances.''

The teenager obviously sensed she'd said something out of place, for the tension that had decreased grew again. But for an entirely different reason.

"If you don't mind,'' L.J. added coolly, "I'd like to get to the trailer and change. My back is beginning to stiffen up.''

"Of course,'' Cooper said contritely. "We shouldn't have kept you.''

"Just because you flattened her like a pancake doesn't mean I get to lose out. Does it, Dr. Livingston?''

The cajoling quality of Mona Channahon got to her. L.J. knew she should refuse. After all, she didn't think much of men who did not take their responsibilities seriously. There was no way Cooper could be anything but the teenager's father. Their resemblance, from the tall, rangy bodies to their light blue eyes and dark brown hair proclaimed their blood relation.

But the girl was not at fault if the man was an irresponsible lout. And he could not be all that bad, from the obvious affection they both shared.

At least he had not totally abandoned his child.

As others so routinely abandoned those who loved them. As her father had done. As Nick had.

Realizing both Channahons were waiting for her answer, and that her back, sore from a week spent in the field, was indeed tightening, L.J. began walking and said, "No. Of course not. You can come tomorrow and observe."

"I want to help out!" Mona said, excitedly clapping her hands.

L.J. looked at Cooper, who nodded his head in silent assent. "Ah, L.J.—May I call you L.J.?," he began, carefully placing his ruined Nikes on the few patches of ground that looked semidry. "About those statements Mona attributed to me—"

"Everyone's entitled to their opinion," L.J. answered.

Cooper noticed her voice was coated with ice, but decided now was not the time to try to explain. He'd rather get Dr. Livingston alone, and tell her—perhaps even show her—that he knew L.J. did have a life.

And one he'd like to be a part of.

"What time will be good for you?" Cooper asked.

"Well, tomorrow is Saturday, but with the weather threatening and the new system coming in, we'll want to get some work in. I'll be out here at 6:00 a.m."

"Six?" Mona gasped, eyes round as saucers. "On a *Saturday*?"

"You have heard of that concept," Cooper teased.

"There is life out there before noon on a weekend, Mona."

"Oh, all right," Mona grumbled. "Anything in the name of science."

Two

An hour later, after a long hot soak in the tiny tub which was her one concession to luxury, L.J. was just wrapping a towel turban-style around her head when a knock sounded on the trailer door.

Thinking it was her assistant, a high school senior named Bradford Palmington whom she was mentoring, L.J. opened the door with a ready smile on her face.

The smile died on her lips and the words of greeting in her throat when L.J. saw who was on the other side.

The man a few steps below her shifted uncomfortably, apparently aware of the change in her expression and the coolness it conveyed.

"Yes, Mr. Channahon?"

"Oh, and here I thought we were on a first-name basis," he said, flashing her a winning smile.

That smile might have melted a lesser woman, but L.J. had had practice toning down the wattage. Being the daughter of a handsome salesman and the ex-fiancée of the college campus heartthrob had given her at least that advantage.

"Just because I was cordial to you in front of your daughter doesn't mean we are bosom buddies, Mr. Channahon."

Even as she regretted her choice of words, the man was going from a knowing look to a frown. Boy, was he good-looking, L.J. silently reflected, steeling herself even further against this unwelcome physical pull.

"Oh, she's not mine," Cooper Channahon was saying.

"She's *not* your daughter?" Now it was L.J.'s turn to frown. That girl was the spitting image of him, and the cretin was denying paternity? "She certainly looks like you."

"Well, that's because—" Cooper Channahon hunched his shoulders against the chilly wind. The feel and smell of rain was in the March air. "Do you mind if I come inside? It's getting awfully cold out here."

"I'm sorry, but yes, I do mind. As you can see,

I'm getting ready to dress and go out. So, if you'll excuse me..."

The man stood awkwardly, obviously not liking this turn of events. But he didn't leave.

Instead, he said hesitatingly, "I realize we didn't get off on the right foot—"

"*You* didn't, Mr. Channahon. My sense of balance is perfect."

"Yes, well, Mona is the one who has the agility of a monkey. I'm much better when I'm off solid ground."

Oh, dear, thought L.J. And he'd seemed so normal. Was he one of the true believers who had come to attend the Aliens and other Paranormals Convention in the farm next to the field she was working on? Heaven forbid!

The APs had already dropped by to try to extract information as to whether preliminary reports of cultural diffusion among her site and the Maya and Aztec were correct.

The disappointment she felt seemed totally out of proportion with the length of time she'd known this man. He was a stranger, after all.

"Mr. Channahon," L.J. began in her teacher's tone.

"What I wanted to say," he said hurriedly, obviously sensing the dismissal and verbal closing of the door in her tone. "I don't want you to take out on Mona any disapproval you might have of me. I'm sorry if you thought I was out of line, I'm sorry I tripped and perhaps damaged some ancient burial treasure and I'm sorry if I stared too long at you. I probably violated every politically correct rule of the nineties, but please, don't take it out on Mona. She's just a child, and she idolizes you."

L.J. was torn between admiration for the man's putting his own child's feelings above his own discomfort, and exasperation at his assumption that she would make a child suffer for the sins of an adult. She knew firsthand what that was like. And even if she hadn't had firsthand experience, she liked children—and respected them—too much to ever use them as scapegoats.

"I meant what I said, Mr. Channahon," L.J. said, her voice as frigid as the rising wind. "Mona is welcome here anytime. And if she'd like, I'll have my assistant Bradford show her some techniques so she can participate in the dig. We can always use enthusiastic volunteers."

Cooper Channahon's eyes brightened. "Hey, that's great! When Mona heard about your dig from her anthropology teacher, she had to visit the site. She's a great fan of yours, and she'll appreciate your generosity."

"Nonsense," L.J. said crisply. "It's rather selfish. Grants are drying up, and funds are being cut all over in this new political climate. I can use all the help I can get."

Obviously the man was not buying her explanation, because he gave her a knowing look. "Knowing fourteen-year-olds, Mona won't be much help to you. But it's nice to give her a job to make her feel important, and let her get a taste of what the field might really entail."

"Wrong on both counts, Mr. Channahon," L.J. said. "This is not a mere 'Let's give the kid some busywork to keep her happy and out of your hair' job. While I always like to raise a child's self-esteem, I *do* have a job to do. And while you may not think much of the field of anthropology and its useful applications in the modern world—" apparently another trait he shared with Nick "—I love what I do. And I also respect a teenager's capacity for work... especially in something that obviously appeals to her so much. I'm merely killing two birds with one stone."

L.J. did not give Cooper Channahon a chance to launch into another apology. She was cold herself, and wanted to blow-dry her hair before she went into Coal City for some groceries.

And dinner.

Her stomach growled just as she was closing the door, and L.J. experienced a momentary embarrassment before her mind moved on to everything she had to do today before she could be ready for further fieldwork tomorrow morning.

* * *

Cooper heard the sound of hunger emanating from L.J.'s stomach, and wondered why he felt so attracted to a woman he had just met.

She was *not* breathtakingly beautiful. She might almost be considered pleasingly plump. Except that her breasts—and he'd had pleasant firsthand knowledge—were on the small side.

His normal preference was for petite, top-heavy blondes. L.J.'s hair was a nice brown, but nonetheless what the guys at work termed "librarian brown." And she was tall. And her green eyes totally devoid of makeup.

Hearing himself cataloguing a very vital, attractive woman's attributes, Cooper winced. No wonder many women considered men Neanderthals.

He had just taken her apart as if she were some car, and had labeled all her advantages as if he were weighing a stock portfolio.

When had he become so jaded and insensitive? He'd beat the guy who would ever discuss Mona in such terms—or for that matter, Corliss, even though he knew full well his younger sister could take very good care of herself.

Shaking his head, Cooper headed toward the car parked on a drier section of land some yards away. He'd picked up Mona from basketball practice straight from work, and his only concession to the surroundings had been to change from his imported leather shoes into the newly purchased sneakers. His suit jacket was no match for the remaining bite of an Illinois winter.

Cooper reached his car and got in with a sigh of relief. He warmed up the car a bit before leaving the site marked DIG IN PROGRESS. Visitors Please Sign In At Trailer Office.

The sign was a rustic, homemade affair that indicated funding was indeed being cut. He'd taken part in a dig back in college to fulfill his science requirements in what he'd considered the easiest way. He'd hated science. But he'd found out anthropology was not easy, nor totally boring. But for someone like him ready to take Wall Street by storm, it had been totally irrelevant.

But even he, with his untrained eye, could see that funding was obviously tight.

Pulling away from the site, Cooper frowned. It had to be really tough having to constantly scrounge to perform one's job. And discouraging.

Yet L. J. Livingston was obviously giving it everything she had.

Cooper could not remember when he'd last felt such enthusiasm for anything—especially his own job as a stockbroker. It no longer seemed a career choice. A highly rewarding job, financially. But a job, just the same.

Accelerating as he reached the main highway— actually, a two-laner, with maximum speed allowed of forty-five miles per hour—Cooper thought of

Mona back in the hotel room. Rather than drive back to Chicago, since they had to be at the site at such an early hour, he'd called his brother and asked him if it were okay if they stayed at a hotel overnight.

Corbett had gladly given his approval. He really needed to get his head together because, although he loved his daughter dearly, he'd not been much of a supportive father lately and had leaned heavily on Cooper to take up the slack.

Cooper wanted to take L. J. Livingston to dinner, but was afraid she'd dismiss the idea out of hand if *he* proposed it. But would the severe Ms. Livingston summarily reject the offer if Mona were involved?

Cooper didn't think so. He had not seen a ring on Ms. Livingston's long, capable finger. And he was sure L.J. would be a stickler for the rules—including wearing a ring if she were either engaged or married.

Any significant others that were not significantly committed did not bother Cooper.

It *did* bother him that he was going to use Mona as a shield when asking the prickly L. J. Livingston to dinner.

But he soothed his own conscience with the knowledge that Mona would love the idea. She already liked going out to dinner with her favorite uncle—since he was an easy touch who let her order whatever her junk-addicted little heart desired.

His niece would enjoy the experience even more with her idol present.

Three

"You really think she'll go for it, Uncle Coop?"

"Monie, unless you call her, we'll never know, will we?" Cooper answered for the third time as he carefully hung his suit jacket on the chair facing the somewhat decrepit desk. He took off his cuff links, and laid them by the tie that was already neatly folded on the desk. He wished he had other clothes to change into, but the best he could manage was a quick shower. Ms. Livingston did not strike him as a woman who spent too much time getting ready. But he had not had a chance to go shopping and get some casual clothes.

Mona moved toward the phone. "What if she says no?"

"Then you go over tomorrow, work your little fanny off and hope she asks you to the site again. And tonight we'll rent movies and gorge on pizza and ice cream."

"You know I can't eat too much junk, now that I'm a starter on the team," Mona began, chewing her lip as she played with the receiver. Seeing storm signals in her uncle's eyes—a rare but definitely serious occurrence—Mona began dialing. "You'll bring me another time if she says no?"

Cooper suppressed a sigh of impatience. Had he ever been such a combination of cocky self-assurance one moment, and then jellyfish indecision the next? Smiling at his niece, he decided, yes, he had. And probably worse.

"Cross my heart and hope to die," he intoned, laughing at Mona's dramatic rolling of eyes.

He went toward the bathroom, getting towels and soap ready—thoughtfully, Mona had asked for fresh towels, as three large fluffy ones lay in total disarray on the bathroom floor—and listened to the conversation briefly. When Mona's eyes lit up like Buckingham Fountain on a clear summer night, he waited...

And watched his niece pump her fists in the air, and jump up and down. Affectionately, Cooper reflected that not only was Mona likely to get a first-class scholarship, but that she could probably play pro ball in Europe—if she wasn't so dead set on

being the next Margaret Mead. Or better yet, Indiana
Jones.

"Where to, Unc Coop?" Mona excitedly cut into
his musings.

"Don't know the area. Ask Ms. Livingston to suggest a restaurant, and we'll meet her there in half an
hour. Unless she wants us to pick her up?"

Unrepentantly, Cooper watched his jumping-jack
niece relay his answer to her idol. It was cowardly,
a truly craven thing to do, but on Wall Street he'd
learned the end justified the means. Anything to pro-
cure that goal.

In this case, not only did Mona's happiness depend
on this, but he was quite willing to ride on his niece's
coattails. Until, that is, Ms. Livingston got to know
him a little better, and he could erase that godawful
first impression he must have made on her.

Once Mona had the details down, Cooper went for
his shower, which set an all-time personal best for
brevity.

"What made you decide to go into the field of
anthropology, Ms. Livingston?" an excited Mona
asked forty-five minutes later.

L.J. put down her glass of red wine and smiled at
the youngster.

"I've always loved learning, and adventure,
Mona. There were so many things I wanted to
study—astronomy, geology, zoology, history...so I

picked the science of man. It encompasses everything and I get to live vicariously every time we discover something of significance, something that allows us to shed light on where we come from, how we got here—and hopefully will help us predict where we are going.''

"But isn't it somewhat boring?" Cooper asked. "I mean, most people think of skeletons and lost mines and rediscovered ancient civilizations, but very few scientists ever find another King Tut's Tomb, King Solomon's Mines—or even a reconstituted T-Rex or raptor.''

"And the real scientist doesn't expect it, nor particularly desire it, Mr. Channahon," L.J. said in even tones. But the look in her eyes as she pinned him to the chair told Cooper Ms. Livingston had seen through his somewhat thin ruse of using Mona to get her to have dinner with him—and didn't think much of his maneuvering, or him.

"Please call me Cooper," he began, but Mona, bless her heart, bridged the awkward moment, and with her youthful tunnel vision, pursued her own interest.

"But that's exactly what *I* want to do," Mona said. "I want to be the next Indy Jones.''

L.J. turned her gaze on Mona, and the green eyes miraculously softened. Cooper felt his chest tighten at the thought of those bedroom eyes trained on him

with less animosity and in more secluded surroundings.

"That's not what a real anthropologist is all about,
Mona," she said softly. "I'm afraid that while the
Indiana Jones series makes for wonderfully enter-
taining films, they cause the serious archaeologist to
shudder at the inaccuracies and careless handling of
what would be priceless relics, had they really ex-
isted."

Mona squared her little chin pugnaciously and
said, "Well, I intend to combine both accuracy *and*
adventure in my work. I'm sure I can rediscover an
Atlantis, or a new mummy's tomb."

"What about your basketball, Mona? Just a year
or two ago you were intent on becoming pro," Cooper reminded her.

"If I do join a woman's league in Europe or South
America, I'll just be postponing my real dream,"
Mona said after taking a sip of orange juice. "And
if I do, it will be only long enough to finance my
education and my research trips and expeditions."

"Well, I'm sure if anyone can accomplish com-
bining Mead, Leakey and Indy into a career, it's
you," L.J. said.

As the waiter approached with a tray laden with
food—most of it Mona's—L.J. asked Cooper, "That
was an astute observation, Mr. Channahon. Have you
ever taken an anthropology course?"

Cooper waited until they sorted out their dinners.

He noticed L.J.'s hidden quick smile at the plethora of plates surrounding Mona like Indians circling the proverbial wagon train in those musty Westerns, and felt his spirits lift. Anyone that attuned to a youngster could not remain unthawed for long.

At least he hoped not. So far, Dr. Livingston did not seem to be responding to what his sister, Corliss, had called his legendary charm.

Which reminded him. "Would you prefer to be addressed as Dr. Livingston?" L.J.'s initial friendliness toward him had deteriorated after Mona's lethal comments, and he wanted to make sure Mona did not overstep her boundaries.

L.J. almost choked on a piece of shrimp. "For heaven's sake, no! Not only does it remind me of that old African Continent chestnut I've had to hear all my life, but it's far too stuffy." Turning to Mona, who was helping tame her spaghetti with a fork and a bagel, she offered, "You may call me L.J."

Mona's eyes lit up, but she waited until she gulped her spaghetti down before saying, "Thank you, Ms. Livingston. I mean, L.J.," she added shyly.

Cooper hadn't seen the shy side of his niece in ages. She really had a bad case of hero worship.

He just hoped that Dr. Livingston—he would always remember their inauspicious beginning, and it was going to take a while for him to accustom himself to thinking of her as L.J.—realized it.

As their eyes met across the table, Cooper saw that

L.J. had, indeed, recognized the extent of Mona's adoration. Her look was less frosty, and her gaze telegraphed reassurance.

Cooper's fierce protectiveness quieted. He had been at the hospital when Mona had been born. His brother, Corbett, had been out of town on business, and because of a blizzard, had not been able to return immediately when the baby had made a premature appearance. Corliss had still been away at school, and Cooper had been at Lauren's and Mona's sides when the doctors had not been sure if either of them would pull through.

As much as he liked L. J. Livingston, he would never let anyone harm Mona or make her unhappy.

Not even a woman he was coming to like and admire as much as L.J.

Mona's piping voice distracted him from those dark hours, a long time ago...

"You stated you were not married, right, L.J.?"

His niece's question alerted all of Cooper's senses. It sounded like the beginning of a typical Mona interrogation.

He knew there had to be *one* good thing about being closely related to a teenager...they really did go where angels feared to tread.

"No, I'm not," L.J. said, her voice laced with amusement.

To disguise his curiosity, Cooper offered her some

more wine, which she declined. He served himself one more glass, and set the bottle down.

"Because I was wondering, like, if you had a husband, or boyfriend, or something, wouldn't it be hard to be here, so far away.... I mean, won't it take you weeks to excavate this site?"

"Months, actually," L.J. answered after slowly chewing some rice. She wiped her mouth delicately with a white cloth napkin, and added, "I wasn't supposed to be here for another few weeks, because of the weather—it's been unusually rainy, as well as unseasonably cold—but I couldn't take a chance with the APs."

"Accounting Programmers?" Cooper asked, perplexed.

Well, that answered one question, L.J. thought. He was *not* one of the Aliens and Other Paranormals true believers.

Smiling, she answered, "I wish that were the case. No such luck. There is a convention of Aliens and Paranormals in the farm field next to the site, and I came down early to make sure they don't disturb anything while chasing and investigating flying saucers and other phenomena. While one of their directors, Serena, seems a levelheaded young woman, the more extreme members keep drilling me as to whether I've found the link with lost civilizations."

"Then it's true?" Mona asked excitedly. "My

teacher, Ms. Thompson, said you were trying to uncover connections to the Maya and Aztecs.''

"It's too early to tell. Supposedly stones depicting Great Temple altars and Maya glyphs were found by some farmers, but we still have to do carbon dating, and ensure that artifacts were not intentionally interred. A certain AP element believe that the Maya were ancient voyagers, and that the lights they sighted in the sky signal their return in their advanced vessels.''

"With the popularity of *Independence Day,* 'X-Files' and 'Dark Skies,' there are a lot of people who seem to believe in UFO's and extraterrestrials. The more ruthless elements could really do some damage,'' Cooper said thoughtfully, pouring the last of the sour cream on a potato already heaping with butter and cheddar cheese. He saw both Mona and L.J. observing him, and added some more butter. He didn't often indulge like this, but watching L.J.'s generous mouth thin with concern for his arteries, he figured he would brave some hardening of his vital vessels if it got him some attention from the aloof doctor.

While L.J. politely refrained from chastising him on his unhealthy habits, Mona had no such compunction.

"Too much cholesterol,'' Mona said with typical teenage inconsistency. Her many plates more than doubled Cooper's intake of heart-sabotaging foods.

"You know Mom said it will be the death of you, yet." To L.J., she confided, "My Mom used to be a nurse."

"Oh, did she change careers? Or did she just want to stay home for a while?" L.J. asked, spearing her last shrimp.

"Oh, neither. Mom died a year ago. A heart attack."

Four

The words were spoken casually, and Mona dug into her fruit salad, picking up her favorite, the pineapple bits.

L.J.'s fork remained frozen on the way to her mouth for an instant. Then she set it down.

The shocked look on her face was quickly replaced with one of concern. Her hand went to Mona's slender wrist.

"I'm so sorry, sweetheart. I didn't mean—"

Mona looked up quickly, and then back down to her salad. She said casually, "Oh, that's okay. You couldn't have known."

L.J.'s comforting hand remained on Mona's for

another instant, her face a study in compassion. It was at that moment that Cooper realized he could easily fall in love with Dr. Livingston.

The thought struck fear into his heart. He had dearly loved Lauren, and had seen the devastation the loss of his brother's high school sweetheart had wrought on his previously carefree younger sibling. Corbett had not recovered yet. He was dazed and confused, daunted before the prospect of raising a teenager without the levelheaded, loving discipline of Lauren.

Cooper pushed that fear aside. Lauren had never been a strong, healthy person. She had been advised against bearing children, but had decided to have Mona at all costs. It had eventually cost Lauren her life.

L.J. seemed a more robust specimen of womanhood. At least, he hoped to God she was. It had been agonizing dealing not only with the loss of a dear sister-in-law, but with the heartache his brother and niece had experienced.

Cooper noticed L.J.'s concerned glance. She was obviously puzzled by Mona's casual attitude. Cooper had been worried at first, too. Mona had never cried.

But Mona was a tough kid. She had obviously resolved her pain and loss in private.

Once again, it was Mona herself who bridged the sudden silence.

"How come you don't have more people helping you?"

L.J. paused while the waiter came over to serve them coffee—Mona decided on a fat-free double-chocolate yogurt—and declined dessert. Cooper asked for an apple pie with scoops of vanilla, strawberry and black cherry ice cream.

At the parallel raising of female eyebrows, Cooper grinned unrepentantly. "Hey, I'm having fruit for dessert! I'm having my vitamin C for the day."

Mona rolled her eyes, and finished the last of her large fruit salad serving.

"The reason I don't have more people helping out, Mona," L.J. answered her, "is that funding is awful tight. I have to beg, borrow or steal to get necessary equipment, money and even qualified people."

"That means you're desperate enough to take on a kid like me?"

"Oh, no, sweetheart," L.J. quickly denied. She seemed to realize belatedly that the endearment had slipped out a second time. A lot of people "deared" and "sweethearted" strangers right away, but L.J. had never been one to instantly assume familiarity.

Mona, though, had brought out her protectiveness right away. Maybe, because in some ways, despite Mona's outward tough-guy image, she reminded L.J. so much of herself at that age—ready to take on the world on the outside, a quivering mass of hurt and insecurity on the inside.

Did Mona's father realize that, too?

From the affectionate look on his face, perhaps he did, also.

"A kid like you, as you put it, is a valuable asset. I've had grown-ups that have volunteered for digs because they thought it'd be a cool thing to do, something to relate at the country club when they got back. But they were not too careful with the pottery, or minimal skeletal findings. And anything resembling garbage, a lot of people refuse to treat as valuable."

"And if I recall correctly," Cooper added, "that is how you tell about the history, living conditions and evolution of a people over time—by the layers of debris accumulation."

L.J. nodded her head, pleased at Cooper's comment. "That's right. So when I run into someone as informed as you, Mona, and as enthusiastic, I know I won't have to constantly remind him or her of how valuable each tiny, seemingly insignificant piece of evidence is."

Mona's flat chest expanded to twice its size. "So you think I'll be of some help?"

"I think you'll be a great help," L.J. said, smiling. "And I've called Bradford, another high school kid who comes in to help me on weekends. He lives in Morton, a couple of hours away, and couldn't make it today. But he'll be there tomorrow, to show you the ropes."

"And how old is this Bradford guy?"

L.J., who seemed surprised at Mona's sudden change of demeanor, answered, "He's a senior. He's seventeen."

"Is he going to lord it over me?"

"Mona!" Cooper gave his niece a stern look. "You're not in charge of this excavation. You're there to give Dr. Livingston a hand, anywhere she sees fit. That's what volunteers do. They help out where needed and take directions from anyone in charge. Got that?"

Mona turned bright pink, and Cooper was sorry he'd jumped at her. But he knew how stubborn his niece could be and did not want her to get in L.J.'s way. Despite what the good doctor had said, L.J. was really giving a high school freshman the chance of a lifetime, and Mona better appreciate it. Mona had always been spoiled, but after Lauren's death, everyone had tread even more softly around her. Maybe too softly.

"Oh, I'm sure everything will go along swimmingly," L.J. said lightly, noting the identical pair of blue eyes locked in silent combat. "But if you don't mind, I have to get going. I've still to organize some things before tomorrow. I'd hoped the article in the daily paper would not have come out for another couple of weeks yet, to allow me to get things in order first, before volunteers and visitors start dropping in."

"We could always come back next weekend, if that would be easier for you, L.J.," Cooper offered.

"No, that's all right. You're here now, and Bradford can instruct Mona in some grid techniques before there are too many people around—most of them gawkers."

L.J. got up, and Cooper followed suit. "Oh, please, just finish your dessert. I hate to eat and run, but I'm really crunched for time."

As she was about to pick up the check, Cooper forestalled her. "Please consider this a donation to the cause." He smiled.

L.J. returned the smile. It was nice to again see the woman hidden behind the serious professor, thought Cooper.

"Thank you." Turning to Mona, L.J. added, "And thank you, too, Mona, for the lovely company and conversation." Including Cooper in her glance, she added, "See you both tomorrow."

The weather was miserable. Mona had not given Cooper too much of a hassle when he'd gotten her up at five, but he'd worried about the drizzling rain and biting wind from the north.

He'd picked up some hot coffee, hot chocolate, bagels and doughnuts from the all-night diner, and had been surprised to find two people in L.J.'s trailer already: one, the high school kid named Bradford

L.J. had mentioned last night, and a second male, which instantly raised his hackles.

L.J. introduced them.

"Cooper Channahon, this is Dr. Roarke Gallagher. Roarke, this is Cooper and Mona Channahon. Mona will be helping out."

As both men sized each other up and stiffly shook hands, both teenagers looked on in wide-eyed interest. L.J. took the bags with drinks and food from Cooper and inspected them.

"Wonderful. We'll actually get to eat well this time. Roarke brought some muffins and fruit, as well as some juice."

"How thoughtful of him," Cooper almost snarled.

"Likewise," Roarke Gallagher answered. His urbane smile revealed a row of perfect white teeth, and Cooper had a sudden urge to rearrange them. Not just the teeth, he reflected, but the smooth cap of straight chestnut hair. And perhaps add the finishing touch of a couple of raccoon rings around those smoky gray eyes, which Cooper was certain many women, bless their misguided hearts, would consider sexy.

The question was, just how sexy *did* Dr. Livingston find Dr. Gallagher?

And more suspiciously, just why had Dr. Gallagher appeared just when Cooper had been ready to stake his own claim?

Turning to L.J., Cooper decided to ask.

"How come Dr. Gallagher so *thoughtfully* decided to drop by on a Saturday morning at six o'clock with some juice and muffins?"

Cooper knew he was being less than civil—heck, he was being downright rude, and he half expected to be told to mind his own business.

He'd never considered himself a jealous man, but the longer one lived, the more one found out about oneself, he told himself with the half of his brain that was not being governed by his raging testosterone level.

The implied question was: Does he do this all the time? And the corollary was, maybe he didn't drop in on Saturday morning, maybe he was already there from Friday night?

"Dr. Gallagher is with a foundation that concentrates its efforts on the Mississippian culture," L.J. replied frostily. "Since the CAA—Center for American Archaeology—has recently flooded, and everything in the museum has been evacuated, he has some free time on his hands. He's a visiting lecturer, but will be doing fieldwork and writing a book on the area—you know, the 'Nile of North America.' His help will be invaluable."

Cooper corralled his baser instincts. From the concern on both L.J.'s and Roarke Gallagher's faces, the flooding was a tragedy.

But he had his own selfish concerns to attend to.

"You know, I was giving some thought to what

you were saying last night, about how you were so short on volunteers. We're having some slow time at work, so I'd like to volunteer my time, too, in the weekends to come." Belatedly remembering to look at L.J., he tore his challenging gaze from Roarke. "If you can use me."

"Oh, we can use any able bodies that are willing to work for free and put in long, arduous hours," L.J. said challengingly.

"But didn't you tell me that with the recession you've got to put in more time at work, because all your clients are having puppies, and you've got to hold their hands while they are having their panic attacks?" Mona asked innocently.

Cooper frowned as both L.J. and Roarke hid smiles at Mona's question. His reason for volunteering, he was sure, was as clear as crystal to Roarke. But now L.J. would think that only out of macho competitiveness, had he volunteered to help her, and that was not entirely true. Besides, Mona's words did not make him sound like a particularly endearing fellow.

"That's not exactly what I recall saying, Mona—"

"Oh, no, you used stronger words than that, but you told me that I'm not allowed to use them myself."

Damn! But it was getting hot in this cramped trailer. And Mona kept digging deeper holes for him.

"You know, the coffee and hot chocolate are getting cold," he said into the loud silence that greeted Mona's latest pronouncement. The child had truly homicidal tendencies.

Roarke was hiding his amusement well, but that kid Bradford had a smirk on his face. There was nothing teenagers liked better than seeing adults busted, and Bradford was getting an eyeful.

Thankfully, L.J. took pity on him and said, "We can use some hot drinks in our tummies before we go out there. It looks like the storm system from the north is going to be joined by the one visiting southern Illinois soon, and we'd better get cracking if we want to get anything done today."

Cooper breathed a sigh of relief as they all moved to the tiny galley to consume breakfast.

Five

Despite their best efforts and intentions, they were not able to get much done before the converging storms from north and south unleashed a torrential downpour on them. The temperature also plummeted, and everyone was forced back into the trailer.

"You know, L.J.," Roarke said, "I've got to get Brad home soon and make it back to Springfield myself. Early tomorrow morning I'm meeting some benefactors regarding possible grants."

"Please don't let us keep you," Cooper said helpfully. He had been downright jealous of the easy camaraderie between Roarke and L.J., and feeling a bit insecure about the fact that they shared a whole world of which he was only vaguely aware. He felt on the fringes of it, and did not like the feeling.

Mona, apparently, was none too thrilled with Bradford Palmington herself. The Channahons were not happy campers.

"Oh, we still have a little bit of time. I'm not going to be able to do anything in Kampsville for quite a while. The rains are predicted for days, so I should be able to help you set up," Roarke said. He turned to Cooper. "Dr. Livingston wants to model this excavation after the Kampsville experience—getting people to dig, but also assist in the laboratory to wash, sort, catalogue and tabulate any materials that might be recovered from the site." Looking at Mona, he added, "L.J. has told me how interested you are in the field. You'll benefit from an interdisciplinary approach in which you'll be able to explore ceramics, paleontology, botany, geomorphology and lithic findings."

"Lithic means stone tools," Mona told Cooper with an air of self-importance.

Cooper refrained from reminding her that he still had some recollection from that dig he'd participated in, and the difficult six credit hours he'd earned. Let her enjoy her moment of glory, even if it meant he had to stand in the shadow of a man he was trying hard to dislike, but not quite succeeding.

"Sounds interesting," Cooper said noncommittally.

"You're in business, right?" Roarke asked as L.J. lifted a box from a corner that was marked Careful! Software! in screaming red letters.

Cooper nodded. "Stockbroker."

"So perhaps you can help set up the computer?" L.J. asked Cooper as he moved quickly to take the box from her hands.

Damn! Cooper thought as he carefully set the box on a table underneath a cheerfully curtained window. They even read each other's minds? Just how well did the two anthropologists know each other? The question gnawed at his gut.

Aloud he said. "Be happy to. Glad to be of help."

Mona found something in common with Brad, who had been trying to impress her with his fount of knowledge: they were both hackers. In no time at all, L.J. had them entering some of her field notes into the main computer that Cooper had hooked up.

L.J. gave Cooper some reading material on field techniques and Hopewell culture.

"I've read about the excavations conducted at Koster by Northwestern University between 1968 and 1978," Cooper said. "I remember that as long ago as 2000 B.C., the forerunners of the Middle Woodland were already adapting native seed plants as crops, even though the bulk from their food still came from hunting and fishing."

"But by 100 B.C. the native crops formed a vital part of the diet, and with the ensuing stability and increased population density, one of the most studied prehistoric cultures in North America emerged—the Hopewell, or Middle Woodland,'' added Brad.

Cooper got up and joined L.J. and Roarke where they were sitting at the other side of the small trailer, talking in soft tones.

"You're studying the culture that follows Hopewell, aren't you?'' Cooper asked Roarke.

Roarke nodded.

"The earliest inhabitants of the area, known as the 'Crossroads of America,' left slight traces of their presence ten thousand years ago. Stone spear points can be found across middle and southern Illinois, and some showed up among the remains of Ice Age elephants.''

"The mammoths and mastodons,'' Bradford supplied.

"Yeah, like the ones on the new stamps the post office put out,'' Mona told L.J., not to be outdone. "Our whole family is into collecting stamps.''

L.J. would have liked to pursue that line of thought—just what exactly *was* Mona's family? Her mother had died, poor baby, but was Cooper involved with someone? A year was usually the interval grieving partners allowed themselves before they began looking for other relationships. L.J. sensed a core of integrity in Cooper, so she was fairly sure he would not be pursuing her unless he was free of any meaningful ties or commitment. And pursuing her he was—he'd made that embarrassingly clear.

But why had Cooper denied paternity of a child who so obviously adored him, and for whom he seemed to fully reciprocate the affection?

L.J.'s line of thought was interrupted by Roarke's deep, smooth baritone. She couldn't help but notice that although both men had sonorous voices, Cooper's was rougher, like stone on silk, while Roarke's was an octave lower. And despite their very divergent professions, in which one would have expected the businessman to be elegant and suave, and the dirt-digging archaeologist to be more informally dressed and coiffed, both men were a study in contrast. Everything about Cooper was rougher, more casual, more out there.

"—and after the conclusion of the Ice Age, the nomadic survivors congregated in the river valleys of the Illinois and Mississippi. The best illustration of this facet of culture is Koster, which as early as 2000 B.C. had developed crops."

Cooper rested slim hips on the table around which Mona and Bradford were entering data, and listened with interest.

Roarke began to pick up the empty cups, juice and muffin containers, and put everything into a large paper bag. Didn't the man have a single vice or weakness? Cooper thought resentfully.

Cooper caught the beaming smile L.J. directed toward Roarke, and he kicked himself for not having thought to help clean up. But heck, as a confirmed bachelor, he'd avoided anything cleaning-related with religious fervor. Noticing how Mona had so effortlessly copied him, bits of muffin and spilled juice trailing in her wake, he frowned. The Channahons were going to go through a neatness makeover.

Lost in his thoughts, Cooper had missed what Roarke had been saying. He caught part of it, and asked, "But didn't the Mississippian culture have a complex society with a ruling class? I seem to remember earthen mounds built in ceremonial centers that contained a few burials of high-status individuals."

"That was the Hopewell. Its more intricate society gave way to a more egalitarian one, and with the advent of corn, which had been diffused from Mexico, the next two hundred years saw witness to the most splendid society in prehistoric North America," said L.J.

"Didn't Cahokia show up at about this time?" Mona put in eagerly.

"Cahokia didn't just show up," Bradford said, turning to face her. His didactic tone obviously ruffled Mona's reservoir of knowledge. She frowned, L.J. thought, in the same endearing way as her father. "The Mississippian culture, of which Cahokia is the greatest example, flourished in the Midwest and Southeast. And Cahokia, begun around A.D. 1000, was matched only by the Inca, Maya and Aztec cities in grandeur and complexity."

"And herein lies the rub," L.J. said. "There are those that hold that these civilizations have a common ancestor—"

"Outer space visitors," Cooper added. "I gather it's not only anthropologists who would like to see a connection."

"You're right," L.J. said, beginning to put away some notes. "Some APs are salivating at the possibility of evidence of celestial navigators, and hounding me at every opportunity."

"Just tell them they're trespassing, and that you'll call the police on them the next time they bother you," Roarke said. Picking up both his coat and Bradford's, he added, "Lesson over for today, ace. I've got to get you home, and then make it to Springfield before the weather worsens." Pulling aside one of the green, yellow and rust-colored curtains, he added, "If that is possible. It looks bad out there."

"Do you want to spend the night here?" L.J. asked, obviously concerned.

Cooper held his breath. Was this a common occurrence?

He released his breath at Roarke's answer.

"No, that's all right. I think we can still make it. But you'd better be careful. Looks like flash floods are a definite possibility."

"I'm on high ground here," L.J. said, linking her

arm through Roarke's, and walking him to the door. "That's why I chose this spot for the trailer."

"Well, you just take care of yourself," Roarke said, bending down a few inches and dropping a quick kiss on L.J.'s lips. Cooper's gut tightened. Just how friendly were they? And didn't the perfect Dr. Roarke Gallagher have any shame, kissing Dr. L. J. Livingston in front of mere children?

Cooper straightened to give himself added height—he'd never quite reached six feet, unlike his strapping younger brother, Corbett, but that fact had never bothered him until today.

Noticing that instead of watching that shameless display of affection between the two scientists, Bradford and Mona had trained speculative glances on him, Cooper endeavored to look casual and unconcerned.

Belatedly he remembered to stop his audible gnashing of teeth.

"Sorry you came all this way. Not only is the weather nasty, but we didn't accomplish much."

"Bradford, let's go," Roarke said, his voice soft, but nonetheless compelling. Cooper noticed that the teenager jumped to attention and gave a quick goodbye to Mona, who barely acknowledged him. Cooper decided he'd have to have a talk with his obdurate niece.

Patting L.J.'s hand, Roarke added, "No trip's a waste if I get to see you. As much as I love our profession and writing, both of them are becoming a bit much lately.''

Poor baby, Cooper thought.

"Well, if you need any cheering up, or someone to use as a sounding board, come over anytime.''

How generous, Cooper thought savagely.

Bradford at his side, Roarke turned to Cooper.

"It was a pleasure meeting you, Cooper. Hope to see you again soon.''

Was that man laughing at him? Cooper could swear that the gray eyes of Dr. Roarke Gallagher were filled with silent amusement.

Squaring his shoulders, Cooper managed to say between painfully knotted teeth, "Likewise. Take care on your drive down.'' *But after dropping the kid off, please wrap your car around a tree. Wouldn't mind having you out of action for a while, while I consolidate my position here.*

As if divining his thoughts, Roarke grinned again, and then, trailed by Bradford, quickly, gracefully, descended the few steps into the quagmire.

Cooper noticed regretfully that Roarke did not trip.

Into the sudden silence that filled the trailer, Mona asked, "Are we spending the night here?''

Cooper's gaze shot to L.J.

No offer to spend the night issued from that quarter, so Cooper said, "No, you have another game tomorrow, and I have to get in some work. We'd better make tracks to the hotel, and we'll get an early start in the morning. Don't forget, it's a three-hour trip."

"Thank you for staying over. I'm sorry you didn't get to work in the field much, Mona, but I'm sure next weekend the weather will be much better."

"Thank you, L.J. I had lots of fun, and I learned a lot."

"Well, now that I have two computer experts to rely on—you and Brad—my job will be made much easier," L.J. said.

Mona's smile was wide and proud. Cooper found his attraction to L.J. growing.

Cooper's gaze was trained on L.J.'s soft, heart-shaped lips, and he only came down to earth when Mona pulled on his sleeve.

"Are you okay?"

Cooper shook himself with an effort. "Yes, I'm fine." Noticing L.J.'s questioning gaze, he added, "Just a bit tired."

"Uncle Coop works too hard," Mona confided as she got her jacket from where she'd dropped it on the floor in a corner of the trailer.

"Uncle?" L.J. asked, surprise evident in her voice.

Cooper, struggling with the zipper on Mona's jacket—she always managed to snag it—said, "Mona's my niece. My younger brother Corbett's daughter."

"Oh!"

Something in L.J.'s tone made Cooper look up.

But before he could say anything, Mona was shoving his own jacket at him. "Come on, come on! If you're going to make me get up early tomorrow, the least you can do is get me a movie and pizza tonight."

Cooper put on his jacket, and was pulled toward the door by a suddenly anxious, blackmailing Mona.

"Wait!" L.J. said. "Here's an umbrella."

"What about you?" asked Cooper as he took the huge, old-fashioned black monstrosity.

"I always keep extras. I'm afraid I'm constantly losing mine."

"Same with old uncle here," Mona helpfully volunteered. "He'd lose his head if it wasn't attached— that's what he says all the time. I just hope he's not getting a case of early senility."

"A little forgetfulness is common, Mona," Cooper said crossly. His niece was making him sound like a prospect for the nearest mental hospital.

"Thank you for coming," L.J. said with a straight face as she walked them to the door.

Cooper felt his heart sink. L.J. was probably glad to be rid of them. He certainly had *not* made a sparkling first impression. But his second impression had managed to eclipse his first.

Saying their goodbyes, uncle and niece made their way down the steps and sprinted toward their car. L.J. noticed how Cooper's arm was protectively curled about Mona's shoulders as he kept them both under the shelter of their borrowed umbrella.

Six

Cooper began stacking all the evidence of Mona's pizza-and-ice-cream orgy as the guilty party lay on her bed and groaned.

"Uncle Coop, why did you make me eat so much?"

Cooper chuckled. "Mona, face it. You take after the rest of the family. You're a bottomless pit. All I have to say is, at your age enjoy it. There might come a time when you might have to watch your weight."

"But I watch it all the time," Mona said, rolling on her stomach, aghast. "Am I getting fat?"

"Relax, tiger. You look marvelous."

"Oh, Unc Coop. You're really out of it. We have to get you a woman, fast!"

"Excuse me?" the horrified uncle said. Pictures of sweet innocent Mona invading the red-light district and picking him up a hooker flashed through his mind. But he knew that once his mad, manic niece put her mind on something, nothing would deter her.

"Yeah, you're getting old and decrepit—"

"Jeez, thanks," Cooper said as he distributed all their junk into the various plastic wastebaskets scattered in the suite.

"—so time is of the essence." Mona jumped off the bed and looked at her uncle consideringly. "You know, you're not a bad-looking guy."

Cooper, about ready to get some papers out of his briefcase for some late-night reading—he'd not anticipated being away so long, and things were quite hectic at work—turned to look at his mercurial niece. "Thanks again. What a wholehearted endorsement."

"But you need to liven up a bit. You're somewhat of a stick-in-the-mud."

Shaking his head, Cooper picked out some files and snapped his case shut.

"I'll do my best to update my stodgy image." He headed for his bedroom, when Mona shrieked, "Oh my God!"

Cooper, alarmed, almost tripped on his own feet, dropping the files on the floor and racing to Mona's side. "Monie, what is it? Are you sick? Hurt?"

Mona shook her head. "No. I'm all right. Physically."

Cooper's heart rate slowed down to about two hundred beats a minute.

"Are you trying to give me a heart attack, Mona? What's the matter?"

"I forgot my textbooks."

"Well, I'll be driving you home before you go to school tomorrow. You can pick them up then."

"No, I mean—" Mona raised big blue eyes and nervously chewed on a nail "—I mean I left them in the trailer."

Automatically removing Mona's hand from her mouth, something he'd done since she was a little girl, Cooper said, "Well, calm down. We'll pick them up before we leave tomorrow. Hopefully L.J. will be up early again and won't be too upset at us disturbing her."

"No! I mean, no, you don't understand. I need them *now*."

"Now?" Cooper looked at his watch. "It's after ten, Monie. By the time I get there, it'll be ten-thirty. I can't disturb Dr. Livingston this late. She said she'd be working tomorrow."

"L.J. works all the time. She'll understand that I need my books for the two exams I have on Monday."

Cooper narrowed his gaze. "If you knew you had two exams coming up, why didn't you skip the movie and the goofing off? And why didn't you tell me earlier, so that I could have picked up your books at a more reasonable time?''

"Well, I needed some R and R. I really did work hard in the trailer, entering all that data and putting up with Mr. Know-It-All Bradford Palmington." When Cooper's gaze remained stern, Mona added, "And besides, Uncle Coop, you were just saying we don't spend as much time together as we used to. You said you missed my being younger, when you had me to yourself a lot more. I just thought you might want to spend some quality time with me.''

Cooper knew a master manipulator when he met one. And he'd been manipulated by *this* master practically since she'd come into the world.

"You are shameless, you know that, mad, manic Mona?''

"And you're the best uncle in the world," Mona said, big blue eyes shining.

Cooper stood there a moment longer, knowing he should be scolding his crafty niece. But she had his number.

Dropping a kiss on the upturned nose, he said, "One of these days, Mona…''

"And you're my *favorite* uncle, too.''

"I'm the *only* uncle you have.''

"But you'd still be my favorite, even if I had a whole bunch of them.''

Cooper put on his jacket again, but ignored the tie.

''Don't let anyone in while I'm gone, and keep

the door locked. And call L.J. and tell her I'm on the way. I don't want her thinking I'm a prowler, or up to some nefarious purpose.''

Mona, ready for bed in her oversize T-shirt, got beneath the covers and looked at him through sleepy eyes. Her rosebud mouth split into a mighty yawn, and she said softly, ''I love you lots, Uncle Coop.''

Cooper felt a gargantuan lump in his throat. When had this bundle of joy managed to put such a stranglehold on his heart, and how could that hold keep increasing year to year?

He couldn't fathom ever being without Mona—or Maggie—and, clearing his throat, admonished his niece once more. ''Come put the safety chain on and lock the door after me.''

Mona got out of bed, and Cooper waited until he heard the sound of locks and chain sliding into place. Walking away, he heard the mattress groan as Mona predictably launched herself onto the bed.

Driving through the dark night and pouring rain, Cooper had time to reflect on L.J.'s earlier comments. Why had she seemed so surprised to learn that he was Mona's uncle? Replaying their conversations in his mind, he recalled that he'd denied being her father.

So she hadn't believed him. Of course! Because of their close physical resemblance, people commonly mistook him for Mona's father.

What kind of impression had he made on L. J. Livingston? Apparently, an even worse one than he'd thought. She'd obviously believed Mona to be illegitimate, and worse, that he was denying paternity.

No wonder she'd looked at him with less than cordiality and friendliness.

Well, now he had the chance to put the record straight. His first two impressions had been big failures. Maybe he could improve his image, sort of grow on L.J.

The constant rain made driving hazardous, and Cooper strained to see through the thick water that curtained him off from the outside world.

Finally making it to the trailer, he was dismayed to see that it was dark.

Maybe the lines were down and Mona had not been able to get through. Maybe the electricity had failed. If that were the case, perhaps L.J. would be happy to see him. And she'd decide to come back with him to the hotel.

Down, boy, he admonished himself. Don't let your fantasies carry you away.

Parking on the highest ground he could find, a small mound near the trailer, Cooper silently thanked L.J. for her foresight, and unfolded the big umbrella before getting out of the car.

His Nike sneakers got another thorough soaking, but by now Cooper was resigned. He'd have to throw these away and get another pair.

A quick flash of light, like a meteor, pierced the darkness.

Cooper paused. Lifting his umbrella, he squinted as he tried to see through the sheet of rain encompassing the landscape.

There! There it was again!

Cooper frowned.

Was he hallucinating? Or had the knowledge of the APs in the field next to L.J.'s archaeological site planted a seed in his subconscious?

He shook his head. This was insane. He did not believe in UFO's, little green men from Mars or any unexplained phenomena. His was a world of logic and empirical proof.

And no one had ever proved beyond the shadow of a doubt that any aliens had landed, or were likely to in the near future.

Hunching his shoulders against the raw wind and castigating downpour, Cooper began walking toward the trailer.

But before he'd taken more than a few steps, something struck him in the back of the knees, and he went down like heavy timber. The umbrella he'd been holding flew from his grasp and made an unscheduled landing a few yards away.

Startled, dazed, his face buried in mud, Cooper felt his arm being twisted behind his back, and a piercing scream rang in his ear.

"L.J.! Call the police! Intruder in the camp!"

The lights went on in L.J.'s trailer, and Cooper shook his head to clear it. He was beginning to get angry.

Very angry.

With a mighty contortion of his upper body, Cooper threw off his assailant and watched the dark-clad body catapult a few feet into the air.

Trying to get up, he discovered that his legs would not cooperate, and swearing fluidly, found himself on his rear end, yet another portion of his anatomy becoming intimately acquainted with mud.

He'd disliked camping and hiking before. He found he hated everything about Mother Nature right now.

"All right, buster. Put up those hands. Nice and easy. No sudden moves."

Cooper looked up into a strong beam of light. L.J. had trained a powerful flashlight on him.

Spitting mud, he croaked, "Dr. Livingston, I presume?"

Seven

"What the hell were you doing out there at this hour?"

Cooper looked from one angry female to another, and sighed.

Women! They were the downfall of men.

First Mona sent him out in the dead of night, then another female attacked him, and now L.J. was letting him have it.

L.J. might be justified but, damn it, he'd had just about enough.

"Mind introducing me to your friend? Batgirl, perhaps? Or Delphina, keeper of the universal flame and peace?"

The woman who'd jumped Cooper flushed through her layering of mud. She obviously had not liked being compared to cartoon characters—especially Delphina, Queen of the Universe, the latest comic-book heroine that was all the rage.

But in her all-black attire, with her flame-red hair contained in Batman-like netting, she really did look otherworldly.

"This is Serena Troy."

"What else?"

"She's one of the leaders of the APs."

"What a surprise!"

"You don't have to look so smug or superior. What were you doing at this hour, skulking in the dark in this weather?"

Cooper ran the towel through his soaked hair, which was still dripping into his eyes.

"I came to get my niece's textbooks. She needs them for her exams Monday." Suddenly angry at the world, Cooper added, "And yes, she's my *niece*. My younger brother's daughter, as I told you. How could you ever think that I would deny paternity, if I had ever been lucky enough to have such a delight for a daughter?"

"I'm sure you're not thinking she's such a delight right now," L.J. said dryly. "And you stood right on those steps just last night, telling me a child closely resembling you was not your daughter. You did not qualify your statement by explaining you were her uncle. I'd apologize to Mona, if I felt it necessary. But even were she illegitimate, it would not be her fault, would it? I don't believe a child is ever a bastard—only those who bring poor children into this world and let them pay for their mistakes and shortcomings deserve such appellations.''

Cooper realized he'd hit upon a touchy subject, and one he intended to explore.

But right now he was wet and sore and miserable.

He wanted a hot shower, but he had no other clothes to change into.

As if reading his mind, L.J. offered, "If you'd like a hot shower, I can give you a change of clothes. I'm sure Roarke's jeans and sweater will fit you."

The thought of Roarke spending the night in this trailer—or any other place—with L.J., sharing her bed, seared through him like a hot poker. The thought of spending a single second in Roarke's clothes made him even hotter.

But it would not do to get pneumonia. Roarke had both the time and opportunity to stick close to L.J. They shared a profession, plus a comfortable relationship.

Cooper did not want that relationship to develop into something even more compelling.

Reluctantly he accepted L.J.'s offer. "Thank you. I'll take you up on both suggestions."

Cooper could not stifle the groan that escaped him as he unfolded his stiff body from the small couch.

Nor could he suppress a few choice words when he found he could not straighten from a right angle. One muddy hand went to his uncooperative back, and he dropped the towel as his other arm instinctively sought support.

L.J. was there instantly to steady him, and he felt strong, sure hands at his back. He stiffened even more when he realized they were Serena's hands on his anatomy.

For cripes' sake, hadn't she done enough harm?

About to tear into Serena, he found that her manipulation was helping. Whatever she was doing to his back was lessening the rigidity and pain.

Slowly but surely he was able to straighten almost completely.

Grudgingly, he said, "Thank you. That helped."

Serena came around to face him. "You're welcome. The least I could do after attacking you. But we have to be very careful. A lot of people don't want us to find the truth."

"The truth?" Cooper asked, nodding thanks as L.J. handed him the towel he'd dropped.

"I'm sure you've seen the 'X-Files'? It's a show about paranormal events and the forces that try to suppress all knowledge. Well, the truth is out there, and the truth *will* come out."

Cooper looked into the almond-shaped blue-gray gaze steadfastly holding his own and could see no signs of dementia there. Still, he'd always held to the belief of avoiding arguments with children or the unstable.

"You obviously have a very narrow mind. But that's all right. Everyone will finally see the light." Turning to L.J., who seemed quietly amused at the exchange, Serena said, "I'll get the umbrella your friend dropped. And I'll also drop by some liniment for his back and knees. They'll both be sore later."

"That's quite all right," Cooper said quickly. "I'll just take a hot shower, and I'm sure I'll be better in the morning."

Serena laughed, a light, contagious sound. "Just ask L.J. if things get better in the morning. She's put in twelve-hour days digging, and twenty-hour days analyzing data. The body needs some assistance in healing itself. But hey, if you insist on being closed-minded about everything, suit yourself."

Serena grabbed her black poncho from a chair near the door and said over her shoulder as she went out, "And next time, why don't you give some advance warning that you're coming, instead of sneaking in late at night? Since some of the members of my group tend to be a bit...*aggressive* about their beliefs, I check on L.J. every day—especially tonight, with the bad weather, and her being alone and all."

Cooper turned to L.J. and said, "I told Mona to call you. It's not her fault that your lines are down."

"My lines? Down? The telephone's working, I'm sure."

L.J. walked toward the telephone that sat on the table loaded with computer, field notes and samples.

About to pick up the receiver to test the phone, it rang, startling both L.J. and Cooper. L.J. answered.

"L. J. Livingston."

L.J. listened and then said into the mouthpiece, "No, Mona. He's all right. He's right here." Looking at Cooper, L.J. added, "That's okay. This is the second time your uncle has had you call me. Maybe he'd better do it himself next time."

Serena came into the trailer, carrying the battered umbrella.

L.J. said, "Hold on a minute, Mona." To Serena she said, "Thanks. Is it still salvageable?"

"I think so."

Serena opened the umbrella with some difficulty and set it on the floor, where it stood looking lopsided and forlorn.

L.J. resumed her phone conversation and said, "Why don't you talk to your uncle? But make it snappy. He's standing in the middle of the trailer, all wet and muddy. If he doesn't want to catch his death yet, he's got to take a hot shower, quick." About ready to hand the receiver over, L.J. frowned. "No, you may *not* do that. You can't stay in the hotel by yourself! Your uncle will be on his way in a few minutes."

Cooper painfully limped to L.J.'s side and took the phone from her. "What's this about you staying in the hotel by yourself?'' Without giving Mona a chance to explain, he said, ''There's no way I'm leaving you alone again, especially overnight. I shouldn't have done it in the first place. From now on, where *I* go, you go!''

Serena, who stood by the door ready to leave, said, ''Why don't I just bring Mona here?'' At Cooper's questioning look, Serena explained, ''L.J. has been telling me all about Mona. It wouldn't be wise of— Cooper, is it?—to go out into this weather again. And he obviously can't let a child spend the night by herself in a hotel.''

To L.J., Cooper said, ''We can't impose on you any further by staying overnight in this crowded trailer.'' To Mona, whose big ears had picked up what her uncle had said, Cooper said firmly, ''No, Mona. And that's final. You've caused enough havoc for one night. You should have remembered your textbooks sooner.''

L.J., although exhausted, found the proceedings highly amusing. She'd even begun to feel the first inklings of sympathy for poor Uncle Coop, when those inklings blossomed to full concern at Cooper's look of dismay.

''Oh, Monie. Don't cry. Of course I'm not upset at you, baby.'' He paused and wiped his face, which was now perspiring from guilt. ''No, I'm okay. No major damage done.''

Cooper missed the look that passed between L.J.

and Serena. He might not have known it, but the two women did.

He was licked.

Serena walked silently to Cooper's side, and waited.

A few seconds later, Cooper turned to L.J. "Would it be too much of an imposition if we spent the night here? Mona says she's heard some strange noises at the hotel, and I can't very well drive over three hours to Chicago at this time of night, in this weather."

Serena stuck out her hand. "Give me the keys to your car. I'll go pick up your niece."

Cooper shook his head. "No, that's all right. I still think the best solution would be for me to skip the shower. Mona won't be afraid if I'm there in the suite with her."

Renewed weeping could be heard emanating from the phone line.

Alarmed, Cooper said into the mouthpiece, "Monie, honey. It's all right. I'll be there right away." He listened for a few seconds then looked at L.J. helplessly.

"I don't know what's going on. She's always been a very brave little girl. She hates crying, and I don't remember her being scared of being alone or of noises or the dark before."

"Well, she did lose her mother a year ago," L.J. pointed out softly. She had a suspicion that Mona

was milking this situation to her own advantage—
she obviously did not want to go back tomorrow,
even if it meant missing her game—but there was
always the possibility that she was having a delayed
reaction to the loss. She might not have dealt with
her emotions when the tragedy occurred, and maybe
Mona had never experienced a sense of closure.

L.J. could not send a child away who might be
frightened and disturbed. Underneath all of Mona's
maneuvering lay a vulnerability that L.J. could not
turn her back on.

"The keys," Serena reminded, her hand still extended.

Cooper looked from Serena to L.J.

The latter, reading the concern and silent questioning in Cooper's gaze, said, "It's all right. Despite
Serena's unorthodox beliefs, I'll vouch for her. She's
a safe driver, and a natural with teenagers. You can
trust her to bring Mona here safely."

Cooper debated silently for another instant and
then dug into his pockets for the rental car keys, telling Serena where they'd been staying.

"Please be careful," he said as Serena grabbed
them and sprinted toward the door.

"Don't worry. I know my way around. And I'll
have your niece back safe and sound, in a jiffy."

Cooper looked worriedly after the door which, before closing, let in a gust of cold rain.

L.J.'s soothing voice reminded him, "Why don't

you take your shower? I'm going to put on some chicken soup to heat, and when Mona gets here I'll make us some grilled-cheese sandwiches.''

As L.J.'s soft tone and words penetrated his veil of worry, Cooper realized something.

His wishes had come true.

He was *alone* with L.J.

Finally.

Eight

A sudden chill shook Cooper's body, and L.J.'s concerned glance went to his face. "I think you've got the beginnings of a temperature."

L.J. put her hand on Cooper's forehead, and indeed, it did feel somewhat warm. His eyes, too, glittered with a touch of fever.

Cooper snared the cool fingers that lay on his forehead, and he shifted them downward so they caressed his cheek, and farther still, so he could press a kiss against them.

He saw the sudden flash of awareness in L.J.'s green gaze, and the rosy blush that stained her cheeks.

Her breathing quickened, and Cooper's gaze was drawn to the nightgown that peeked out from underneath L.J.'s robe. She'd obviously been in bed when he'd arrived, and had just thrown on the robe and a coat before venturing outside in answer to Serena's yelling.

Pulling on the hand that he held captive, Cooper slowly, inexorably drew L.J. to him.

Both stopped breathing in unison, and their trapped breaths comingled when Cooper's mouth hungrily swooped on L.J.'s.

His other arm went around L.J.'s waist, and he pulled her to him, fitting her curves more intimately to his, forgetting for an instant that he was soaked through and through.

The sensual shock of Cooper's invasion, his lips opening hers up and his tongue delving within to mate with hers almost obscured the second shock of his body molded to hers. But the wet and cold of his clothes insinuated themselves into L.J.'s barely conscious mind.

A moan escaped from L.J.'s depths, and it was swallowed by Cooper, whose lips, teeth and tongue were a trinity of sensation, robbing L.J. of any willpower and infusing her with a fire that had lain dormant for too long.

But the strength of her need, and the extent to which Cooper had tapped into it scared her.

Twisting her head, L.J. escaped the source of the

flames that were consuming her, and dragged her throbbing lips away from Cooper's.

For an instant, they both stood there, trying to recover both their wits and the oxygen that had seemed so unnecessary seconds...or was it aeons...ago.

"You're going to come down with the flu," L.J. reminded Cooper, who looked as stunned as she felt.

Her voice was throaty, sexier than usual. Her cheeks were coral, her lips red and sensually swollen, and her eyes emitted emerald sparks.

She looked absolutely, ravishingly beautiful, Cooper thought.

As his eyes took in the wet imprint contact with him had left on her chest, her heaving breasts, their tips proudly erect underneath the damp material, he told her so.

"You'd better take that shower," L.J. said, choosing to ignore this compliment. And the lambent light in his gaze.

"I'd better make it a cold one," Cooper said ruefully.

L.J. crossed her arms across her chest, and seeing the protective movement, Cooper was flooded with remorse.

"I'm sorry. This is no way to repay your hospitality. You've gone beyond the call of duty for my niece, and now her uncle accosts you—"

"Let's forget it, shall we? You stayed here to

avoid catching pneumonia, so you'd better get into that bathroom and warm up.''

The instant the words were out of her mouth, L.J. regretted them. Cooper certainly did not need anything to warm him up.

He'd been burning before.

But Cooper bypassed the opportunity to remind her of his—and *her*—body heat.

Instead, with a rueful smile, he grabbed the clothes L.J. handed him and went into the small bathroom for his delayed shower.

L.J. shook her head and rubbed her neck wearily.

How could she have been so foolish as to forget? Even for a moment.

Granted, she was exhausted. She'd been running on willpower for a very long time.

She'd temporarily given up her post at the university and had found someone to take over her classes so she could watch over the site.

It had been a long road to get permission from the absentee owners to set up an excavation at the site. Even more harrowing had been her effort to secure funding. In this political climate, when the arts and sciences were being hailed as expendable, L.J. had found increasing resistance to what she now viewed as a crusade.

A one-woman crusade, it seemed.

She had learned to stay away from charming, handsome men.

She had not been celibate, by any means. But the relationships she'd engaged in had been mostly platonic, and those that had gone beyond friendship, she had made sure could not get to the point where it would hurt to say goodbye.

Not only did she not have time at this point in her life to become heavily involved—not if she wanted this excavation to be conducted properly and thoroughly—but men like Cooper were dangerous.

He had to be close to forty, yet he seemed to be without a commitment.

He so mirrored her father and ex-fiancé in looks, charisma and life-style, that she should have *known* better.

She was no impressionable teenager, no adoring, doting daughter trying to please either a man, or her father.

She had a life to lead, and she intended on doing it alone.

It hurt a lot less that way.

Even if it was unbearably lonely sometimes.

By the time Cooper emerged from the bathroom, L.J. had managed to pull herself together, had the soup on the stove, and had set the makings of her famous grilled cheese, bacon, lettuce and tomato on the counter.

Cooper, Serena and Mona could choose any variation thereof.

"That looks delicious," Cooper said over her shoulder.

Although wanting to move skittishly away, L.J. held her ground.

She looked into Cooper's eyes. They were almost of a height, since she was five ten, and Cooper a shade under six feet. "Thank you."

She saw Cooper's frown. If he expected to resume where he'd left off, he had another thing coming.

She was a professional with a job to do. She'd let herself be sidetracked by a charming teenager and the girl's equally charming uncle.

While not sorry about becoming involved with Mona, L.J. was on guard against Cooper. He'd demonstrated a depth of caring and affection that Nick had never evinced.

L.J., in her youth, inexperienced and lost in a world of new, sensual delights, had believed Nick truly loved her. But Nick had only loved himself, and she'd been devastated when they'd broken up.

But Cooper really did care about his niece and family. So she had to be doubly careful not to become entangled with him, because if sex had been great with Nick, it was bound to be all-consuming with Cooper.

And it would go a lot further than sex.

L.J. was determined *not* to lose her heart again.

"Would you like to eat now, or wait for Serena and Mona to get back?"

"Oh, I'll wait. Anticipation makes reality even grander, don't you think?"

L.J. smiled, noticing the challenging light in Cooper's aquamarine eyes.

"Well, I've always believed that control was the root of all power. So I guess we both agree on principle."

Cooper's gaze narrowed. He seemed to sense that L.J. had adopted another strategy, but he wasn't sure what it was. And he was carefully testing its boundaries.

Before he could get a full bearing on the situation, L.J. asked him, "Would you like some coffee while you wait?"

"Thank you, I'd love some."

L.J. poured some coffee into her favorite mugs, each a reminder of digs or expeditions she'd been on, ranging from Mount Fuji in Japan, to Chichén Itzá in Yucatán, to the Pampas in Argentina.

"Interesting cups," Cooper told her, resting his tight, luscious buns against the tiny kitchen counter, and aggressively leaning toward her in the small confines of the kitchen. Roarke's casual jeans and shirt did not diminish Cooper's raw, powerful appeal.

Cooper, too, was sending a message. Loud and clear. While he'd obviously been sorry for taking advantage of her hospitality, and would refrain from inopportune advances, he was not about to discontinue his pursuit of L.J.

L.J. held her ground, again, and concentrated her scattered thoughts on the cups in question.

"Everywhere I've gone, I've tried to bring back souvenirs from the field. But since I can't very well keep a flint chip or ceramic vase with me—they belong in museums or universities—I've picked up cups that are daily reminders. And I take them on every extended field study."

"Have you broken any?"

"A couple," L.J. admitted. Grinning, she added, "But I've covered myself. I try to buy a few cups each time so I can replace the occasional one that inevitably does not survive the rigors of cramped quarters and visiting volunteers."

Cooper smiled back. L.J. reflected that his teeth were not as perfect as Roarke's. But then, Roarke's smile did not send her heart and pulsebeat into overdrive.

Realizing the evocative smell of soap and sexy male was getting through her defenses, L.J. moved away from Cooper and began setting the table.

It might be a defensive maneuver, but L.J. decided she'd rather lose some small battles but win the war.

Because defeat in this campaign for her heart would surely be costly. And deadly.

"Here, let me help you," Cooper said, taking the plates from L.J.

Their hands brushed, and their gazes met.

Cooper's head began descending toward hers, but stopped in midmotion as the door to the trailer crashed open to admit two drenched figures.

Although Mona had been responsible for much of what was happening, L.J. had never been so glad to see anyone in a long, long time.

Nine

"Hi, Uncle Coop! Hi, L.J.! Did you know, Uncle Coop, that Serena is codirector of the APs? She was telling me all about their national organization. I think I'd like to belong to their local chapter and—"

"Mona, get out of those wet clothes and sit at the table, please. Despite all the trouble we've caused L.J., she has very graciously prepared us a late meal."

One look at Cooper's stormy expression, and Mona quickly got out of her jacket, took off her sodden sneakers and took her place at the round table.

Serena came forward to hand the keys and a small bottle to Cooper. "I made a quick stop at my site to get you the liniment. I always keep some in my trailer.''

Looking dubiously at the bottle in his hand, Cooper thanked her.

''Your car is parked on that small mound. The rain is starting to let up a bit, so it and the trailer should be okay tonight.''

''What would you like, Serena? A grilled cheese, or your usual bacon and tomato?''

''Thanks, L.J. But I'd better get back.''

''Let me pour you a cup of hot soup before you leave.'' L.J. rushed to the cupboard and extracted a thermal mug. ''It's the least I can do after all the trouble you went through.''

''L.J. makes the best chicken soup in town,'' Serena said, taking the container from L.J. Pulling on her hood, she addressed uncle and niece. ''Nice meeting you, despite the circumstances.'' To Mona, she offered, ''Come by anytime. If your uncle allows it.''

Cooper got up to see Serena to the door. ''Thank you again for picking up my niece. My knees and back will never forget our first encounter. I'll make sure to always look over my shoulder from now on whenever I approach this area.''

Serena's crystalline laughter remained in the air after she launched herself down the steps. ''See you...''

Cooper closed the door behind her after taking a

quick look outside. As Serena had said, the storm seemed to be losing its voltage.

Resuming his place at the table, Cooper addressed his wayward niece.

"Why didn't you call L.J. right away like I asked you, Mona?"

Mona took her time answering, eating some of the soup L.J. had served. "This is really good, L.J. I haven't had such tasty chicken soup since my mother died. Uncle Cooper is not much of a cook, and my dad has been pretty helpless since Mom's been gone."

Some of the fire left Cooper's eyes. L.J. could tell that Mona had achieved her objective. By reminding her uncle of her grave loss, Mona had effectively defused the situation.

It was a touchy predicament. On the one hand, Cooper did not want to be heartless. The child *was* motherless.

On the other hand, how often had Mona used such an excuse to get away with practically murder?

Spooning her own soup, L.J. waited to see what Cooper would do.

"I'm sorry I'm such a bad uncle and rotten cook, Monie. You know I've always tried to do my best by you."

Thrown for a loop, Mona looked at Cooper uncertainly.

"And you do, Uncle Coop. I know you try to do your best."

"And I'm sorry that being with me was such a trial to you that you tried to get rid of me in the hotel, and then couldn't stand the thought of spending another night in my company."

Now obviously laden with guilt, Mona said, "But that's not it at all, Uncle Coop. You know I enjoy being with you. And I guess I'd better start learning how to cook. But Dad told me that I don't like being in the kitchen too much, that I'm like Aunt Corliss who hates housework, and that if I'd rather pursue other interests than domestic ones, that I should be free to do whatever I want, even if it's not a typical or traditional female pursuit."

"I'm not criticizing you for not knowing how to cook, Monie," Cooper said calmly. "You were just saying how bad a cook *I* was, remember?"

Mona frowned. "Well, yes, but I—"

"But you thought you'd get out of the early game tomorrow and maybe school Monday, and made us all go through such a circus. Don't you think that was rather a selfish thing to do? Not only am I responsible for your safety, and liable to your dad should anything happen to you—and by God, *should* anything happen to you, I don't know what I'd do— but you put two other people through a lot of bother. And L.J.'s time is already severely strained. Your volunteering was supposed to help ease L.J.'s problems, not increase them, Monie.''

About to say something, Mona apparently thought better of it. "I'm sorry, L.J. I guess I didn't think. I didn't mean to cause such a commotion. I know you need your rest, and that you've been working hard—"

"No more than your dad and uncle, I suspect," L.J. said, serving Mona some more soup. "Apology accepted. Just tell me what kind of sandwich you'd like."

Looking from L.J. to Cooper, Mona resumed eating her soup. "I really am sorry, Uncle Coop," she added when her uncle's expression had not cleared entirely.

Cooper obviously had more on his mind, but thankfully he refrained from adding anything else. L.J. thought that Mona had been properly chastised and that things should be dropped.

After another tense minute, Cooper began eating some soup and said, "I'd like the whole works on my sandwich, if you don't mind. I find I'm famished."

"Me, too," Mona said happily. "I'm starving to death."

"So what else is new," Cooper said, ruffling his niece's damp hair.

L.J. felt a sob rising in her throat, and determinedly pushed it down. She remembered how much such casual gestures of affection had meant to her when she was young. Because her father had been away so much, they'd been few and far between.

But they were tucked away in the precious album of her memories, and she hoped both Mona's uncle and father realized that although teenagers might act as if being touched by a relative were the grossest thing in the world, deep down inside they needed that affection, that tactile reassurance that their topsy-turvy world, with mercurial changes in body and emotions, was still a safe, warm place to inhabit.

A half hour later they were done with their late meal, and were more than ready for bed.

The question was, where would she put them?

"Mona could take the couch. It's not very big, but she could let her legs hang over the edge," L.J. suggested.

"Oh, I can sack out on the floor. I do it all the time on sleepovers," Mona said, covering the mighty yawn that scrunched her cherubic face.

"I'll take the floor, you get the couch, Mona," Cooper said, brooking no argument.

"I'll get the extra blankets," L.J. said, going to a hope chest that was hidden by the latest archaeology reports, magazines and comparative studies.

"I didn't know they still had those," Cooper said.

"This one belonged to my mother," L.J. said. "I found that it traveled well when I went to foreign countries, and it also protected fragile items or things of sentimental value.''

"So it goes with you, just like the cups," Cooper told her as he took the two blankets and extra sheets from her. "Sort of a home away from home."

L.J. smiled. "That's right. Months on the field, working with new volunteers all the time, can wreak havoc on you, especially when you meet so many wonderful people and realize, as you say goodbye, that in all probability you'll never see them again.''

Cooper looked thoughtful, but whatever he was about to say was lost when Mona asked sleepily, "Can I have an extra pillow?"

"Well, I've only got two, so one of you will have to go without," L.J. said, looking from niece to uncle.

"Give it to the princess," Cooper said. "I can make do with a makeshift one."

L.J. went to her bedroom to get the pillow, and brought back a long robe and extra blankets. "You can roll this up, if you like. It's soft material, and ought to help out a bit."

"Great! Sorry for the imposition, L.J.," Cooper said, taking the robe from L.J.

Their fingers touched, and L.J. felt the electricity jump from his skin to hers, traveling up her nerve endings and awakening every cell in her body.

But Cooper, knowing Mona's eyes were sleepily but hawkishly watching them, merely smiled.

"We'll be up at four tomorrow, and will be out of your hair for good."

"Four! But I thought we'd get to stay here a couple extra days!" an indignant Mona said, sitting up in her too-small makeshift bed.

"You thought wrong, Monie. You seem to forget I have a job and a lot of work to catch up on. And *you* have a game and school, too."

"Yeah, but it's midnight now, and I'll get less than four hours of sleep. There's no way I can play basketball tomorrow, and study for my exams in this condition," she complained.

"You've gone without sleep before, Monie. And besides, you should have thought of that before you put yourself in this predicament."

"Mona could stay here tomorrow, if you'd like," L.J. offered. "You could pick her up after work, and take her home then."

"Yes, please, Uncle Coop. May I, may I?" Mona asked beseechingly.

"Absolutely not," Cooper said firmly. "You can come back next weekend—if and when you behave. Now you'd better get to sleep quickly, because I'll be waking you up before you know it. Don't forget we have to stop by the hotel to check out and for other last-minute details before heading back to Chicago."

Mona grumbled under her breath and pounded the pillow. Cooper went over to rearrange the blanket, and dropped a kiss on the soft, dark hair. Mona twisted to face her uncle, and kissed him on the cheek.

L.J. watched as Cooper tenderly smoothed the strands that were getting into Mona's eyes, and felt that telltale clogging of her throat.

She was really getting sentimental in her old age!

But she had always thought that there was nothing on this earth sexier than a man who was gentle and affectionate with children.

And Cooper seemed to possess both qualities in abundance.

"Good night," L.J. said softly. "Don't let the bed bugs bite."

"Good night," Mona answered sleepily, the sound muffled against the pillow as she got comfortable on her stomach.

L.J. smiled at Cooper and headed toward her small bedroom.

She sensed rather than heard Cooper follow her, and turned just as he crossed the threshold. Cooper stared at her in the soft illumination from her bedroom lamp, his gaze filled with longing and passion.

L.J.'s breath caught in her throat. She waited for she knew not what, realizing it was madness to get involved with Cooper, yet responding to the need and hunger she read in his expression and sensed in the tight control he held over his body.

With effort, Cooper relaxed his body, and his look turned to one of gentleness.

"Thanks again for everything, L.J.," Cooper told her, his eyes making silent love to her.

Then he turned and went to the kitchen, where he moved the table, made his bed and turned off the only other light still on in the trailer.

L.J. finally remembered to breathe and to move.

Closing the door on the Channahons, L.J. took off her robe, laid it on a chair and set her alarm clock before climbing into a cold, suddenly lonely bed.

Ten

The shrill sound of the alarm buzzed through L.J.'s brain the following morning.

At first she could not recall where she was.

Then Cooper's image invaded her conscious mind and she jumped out of bed, throwing on her robe as she walked out of the bedroom.

The welcome aroma of coffee greeted her but made L.J. feel even more alone than ever.

The blankets, sheets and pillow were neatly arranged on the couch.

Cooper and Mona had left already.

He'd obviously meant the part about getting out of her hair.

But he had not realized—nor had she—to what extent she'd be missing the pair.

Sighing, L.J. scolded herself as she moved to the kitchen, and while she poured herself a cup of the coffee that Cooper had thoughtfully left warming on the stove and that was as strong and sure as the man himself, L.J. told herself this was what she wanted. No involvement, no complications.

Besides, she had a lot of work to do.

Swallowing down the hot brew and waiting for the caffeine to do its trick, L.J. checked the weather. It was chilly, but not unseasonably so.

And it had stopped raining.

Some juice, an English muffin and another cup of java, and she'd be ready to start the day.

Funny how a few days ago she'd been content and appreciative of her independence and freedom.

Now she found the trailer a lot bigger, and a lot emptier.

It was a natural phenomenon, L.J. told herself, experienced by everyone who'd had houseguests.

L.J. ignored the voice that reminded her that she could not wait to get rid of many a houseguest in the past.

Well, it wouldn't be long before she'd see Mona again, L.J. reminded herself. It'd be nice to see her uncle, too.

But Cooper was strictly off-limits, L.J. admonished herself. He had given no indication of wanting any long-term relationship.

And L.J. had survived all these years by avoiding heartache.

She'd better get used to being alone. She'd liked it before and she would love it again.

Later that day, Serena dropped in for a visit. She'd baked several pies—apple and cherry—and had brought one of each to L.J.

"You'll be the death of me yet," L.J. told Serena as they both sat at the small table in the kitchen.

"Why, don't you like it?" Serena asked as she served herself a second slice of cherry pie—a *very* large slice.

"You know I do, you evil person. That's just the point." Savoring the thoroughly baked apple which was sinfully rich with brown sugar and cinnamon, L.J. scolded, "How can you put away such enormous quantities of fattening food and still stay so slim? And on top of it, you're mean enough to tempt me with one of my favorite desserts."

"For one, traveling all over the country in search of proof of UFO's and other paranormal phenomena gets kind of lonely. Baking pies in strange places gives me a sense of home, of connection. And secondly, it wasn't only you I was thinking of," Serena defended herself. She poured herself a glass of milk—she never drank coffee, tea, pop or anything containing caffeine. "I thought Mona and her uncle would still be around. That man really has the hots for you."

Startled, L.J. stared at Serena. "What do you mean?"

"Oh, come on!" Serena finished her glass of milk, which left a white mustache on her full upper lip. "Didn't you tell me that Cooper seemed ready to jump his rival Roarke at the slightest provocation. And are you going to tell me that if that adorable niece of his wouldn't have been around, that you wouldn't have engaged in some nice hanky-panky with her gorgeous uncle?"

L.J. got up from the table, and went to get herself some more cream for her coffee.

"You know that Roarke and I are just good friends and we respect each other professionally. As for the rest, I don't know what you mean," she denied. But her denial held no conviction, and as she returned to the table, L.J. saw an infuriatingly knowing smile on Serena's face.

"If you say so." Apparently realizing L.J.'s reluctance to discuss her attraction to Cooper, Serena changed the subject. "Have any of my people been bothering you lately? I know you said when we first met that you'd experienced some trouble with other APs at another site you were working on."

L.J. served herself a second portion of apple pie, this time a smaller slice, and nodded. "I've seen a couple of your people trespassing, and I've had to get rid of another pest who persisted in prying me for information I have yet to confirm or deny. These are just the early stages of excavation. I'm sure they don't mean any real harm, but sites have to be protected against outsiders, even if they are not malicious. If we are lucky enough to have archaeological evidence that has survived the centuries, we have to make sure these fragile testaments of time endure careless and uninformed trespassers.''

Serena poured herself some more milk, gulped it down and got up. "I'll talk to my codirector. He's not the most rational of people, and he tends to go off the deep end. Which is why I made sure I had some say-so at this convention. Because after this gathering is over, my core people of 'UFO-chasers' and I will remain, and we don't want any laws broken, or anyone harassed."

L.J. walked Serena to the door, glad for the short break from work and the companionship she'd provided.

"You were saying that you've been looking for a permanent site for psychic experimentation?"

Serena nodded. "For a long time. We're like those other nomads, the storm chasers. The farmer who's letting us use his land at a nominal cost is also a believer. And this would be a perfect spot for a headquarters, a place to keep our research, computers—heck, a real 'home' base. If some members of my group don't self-destruct. We have enough problems with attacks and misunderstanding by the outside world without collapsing from within.''

Stepping outside the trailer, Serena added, ''But hey, I didn't mean to unload on you. I know you have enough problems of your own.'' Pulling the edges of her coat closer to her throat against the increasing chill of late afternoon, she asked L.J., ''If that little firebrand Mona shows up again, let me know, okay? I really like the girl, and I did promise her a tour of our compound.''

''Sure thing. And thanks again for the company and goodies.''

Serena's answering smile was melancholic. ''I know we don't agree on principle, but I think we have a lot in common, L.J. We're both after the Holy Grail, so to speak, only searching for it from different perspectives and time frames—you delving into the ground and the past, me looking to the skies and the future.'' Shivering, she pulled on her hood. ''And while we both have the same difficulty acquiring funds, at least you're part of the establishment, a recognized academician, while I'll always be on the fringes, a New Age freak.'' Shaking off her pensiveness, Serena gave L.J. a quick hug. ''Do me a favor, will you? Give 'Uncle Coop' a chance? Guys like him are few and far between, and the road we travel tends to get longer and lonelier as time goes on.''

* * *

Serena's words stayed on L.J.'s mind the rest of the day and week.

On the one hand, she felt ashamed of her shallowness and prejudice. True, she didn't believe in UFO's, but she had always thought herself a fair, open-minded person.

Yet she remembered her reaction when Serena had shown up at her door shortly after she'd arrived to set up camp, carrying a little plant and one of her famous pies.

Although she'd tried to hide her dismay, L.J. must not have been quite as successful as she'd thought. She'd quickly invited Serena in after she'd introduced herself as one of the codirectors of the neighboring, upcoming AP convention, thanking her for her welcoming gifts.

But now L.J. realized that her reaction, while perhaps less harshly disapproving than others—she still considered many true believers loopy—must have been something Serena had encountered over and over.

Yet Serena still had the courage to stick by her beliefs, and the decency and warmth of heart to offer friendship even when it might be rejected.

What a lonely life Serena must live!

And while L.J. did not consider her plight as triste as that of her new friend, would she, years from now, recall this conversation, and wonder about the road not taken, the chance passed up?

L.J. had not been willing to be open and totally honest with Serena, in part because she was not sure of what her unfolding feelings were.

But the minute she'd met Cooper, she'd sensed something exciting between them, the potential of something deep.

Which had scared the heck out of her, and her carefully planned and protected life!

Would she really have engaged in "hanky-panky", as Serena had intimated, if Mona had not been present or been an inhibiting factor?

L.J. liked to think she would not have, that she had enough maturity and self-control to have conducted herself professionally and with the utmost decorum.

Of course, the point was moot, since Mona was the catalyst that had brought her and Cooper together.

But she remembered the passion of Cooper's kiss and, even more alarming, the power his gaze and mere presence had over her as he'd stood inside her bedroom.

L.J. was full of consternation at the thought that if she weren't careful, Cooper could easily steal her heart.

And Serena's advice notwithstanding, L.J. decided as her heart once again recalled the pain from the past, she had to be doubly careful to prevent him from doing so.

* * *

That determination carried her until Friday morning, when once again, she got up at five to continue delineating the different areas of the site her volunteers would work on, and to transfer that information into her computer.

She'd been working outside steadily for four hours when she heard the sound of footsteps crunching on the ground behind her.

L.J. paused, thinking it was Serena or one of the members of her group.

Getting up from her kneeling position, she turned to face her visitors.

And came face-to-face with Cooper.

Standing right behind him, a triumphant smile on her face, was Mona.

The teenager, never at a loss for words, filled in the chasm of silence the adults did not bridge.

"How are you, L.J.? I convinced Uncle Coop to bring me over for a three-day weekend. Can you use our help?"

Eleven

After L.J. put Mona to work on a small grid—complete with instructions and admonitions to be careful and thorough—she went back to her trailer to get herself a snack and something to drink.

Mona had already indicated her willingness to digest anything available, so Cooper went back with L.J. to ostensibly help her carry the drinks and sandwiches.

"Seems all you do is feed us and put us up for the night."

L.J.'s eyebrows made perfect quarter moons.

"Not put you up tonight, surely? You have made arrangements at the local inn?"

Cooper chuckled. "Yes, I have. As soon as my darling niece had blackmailed me into bringing her here a day early, so she can get extra credit for the honors anthropology class she's taking."

L.J. walked quickly, pleased that Cooper was able to keep up. With her height and long legs, she found she had to adjust her speed to whoever was accompanying her, and it made her impatient.

She laughed, and Cooper asked, "Something I said?"

"No. I was just thinking that you're able to keep up with me. Most people slow me down, and I was mired in self-pity, thinking that there is so much to do and so little time...."

"Well, I agree with the second part of your statement, especially in view of the fact that this is basically a one-woman operation, so far," Cooper said, sprinting up the steps to the trailer to open the door for L.J. "But as to the keeping up with you, I must admit, while a daunting prospect, I'm willing to give it a try."

L.J. shook her head at Cooper's wicked grin, and preceded him into the trailer. She could feel his eyes on her backside, but did not feel the least bit self-conscious. After all, she'd ogled his tight behind, too, and she was confident in her rear end. It, and her legs, were her best features. Below her neck, that is, she silently amended, feeling herself blush as her thoughts strayed to Cooper's below-the-neck attributes.

"A penny for your thoughts," Cooper requested as L.J. washed her hands at the sink.

"Sorry. Not for sale." She passed the soap to Cooper, and began setting up the makings for ham and Swiss cheese sandwiches on the table. "Does Mona prefer American cheese?"

"Please, don't coddle her so. Swiss will be fine. I'm afraid between her father, aunt and myself, we've spoiled her far too much."

L.J. wanted to ask about the rest of Mona's—and Cooper's—family but they still had a lot of work to do. She also felt she'd better steer away from personal subjects. That way, Cooper would not feel free to ask her a lot of personal questions also.

"You said Mona is taking an honors anthropology class?" L.J. asked Cooper instead. "I didn't realize it was standard high school curriculum for freshmen, which I assume Mona is."

"Mona just turned fourteen, but she *is* a freshman, and no, it isn't standard. Seniors may choose it, but Mona has always been an outstanding student, and she asked for permission to take it instead of general science."

Cooper washed the lettuce and tomato for L.J., while she laid out the ham and cheese on the wheat bread. Before lightly using the mayo, L.J. asked, "Mustard instead?"

"Mayonnaise will be fine," Cooper answered.

"But general science will come in handy, too, if Mona intends to pursue a bachelor of science in college."

"I know," Cooper answered, watching as L.J. quickly, artfully, arranged the meat, cheese and veggies on the bread and then covered each individually in plastic wrap. "But she'd read some articles on you in *American Anthropology* and *Women in Science,* and had wanted to be prepared in case you'd allow her to sit in on one of your seminars on Women and Anthropology."

L.J. paused in the act of wrapping her last sandwich. For easier eating, she'd cut each sandwich into precise quarters.

"I admire her dedication and advance planning, but I hope she doesn't put me on a pedestal. I am a scientist, have worked my butt off on my doctorate and postdoctoral studies, and I live and breathe anthropology, but I am *not* perfect."

"Who is?" Cooper said, taking an ice tray out of the refrigerator and emptying it into a cooler. "But I'm afraid you can't escape your pedestal. You're Mona's idol, just like thousands of little astronauts-in-the-making revered Sally Ride."

L.J. groaned, and arranged the sandwiches and some already neatly cut up veggies and fruit into the cooler.

"Haven't you disabused her of the notion? As her

uncle—and an obviously adored one—your word ought to carry some weight.''

"I'm afraid you've got us both in your thrall, Dr. Livingston,'' Cooper told her huskily.

L.J., in the process of closing the cooler, froze.

Cooper closed the distance between them and put both hands on her waist. They moved around to the small of her back, where they massaged with practiced skill, and then slid upward along her spine, causing all sorts of deliciously wicked sensations to travel up her vertebrae.

Suddenly cotton-mouthed, L.J. instinctively licked dry lips.

Cooper moved with killer instinct, capturing the pink tip of her tongue with his teeth, and biting down gently.

All systems ceased functioning in L.J., and then roared back to life. Cooper's fingers tangled in her hair, which lay in disarray about her face and neck, and he sucked on her tongue, almost swallowing her whole.

At least that's what L.J. felt. She felt consumed by Cooper, by his magnetism and virility. One hand remained in her hair, massaging her scalp, while the other moved downward to cup her bottom and press her more intimately against him.

She was drowning, drowning in desire....

And Cooper was masterfully tugging her into a

maelstrom from which, in another second, there would be no escape.

With an incoherent sound, half moan, half denial, L.J. fought the whirlpool dragging her under, and used the lid of the cooler she still held in her hand to push Cooper away.

For an instant—a brief, time-devouring instant—Cooper did not budge.

Then he lifted his head and moved slowly away from her.

L.J. began breathing again, her oxygen returning to her lungs in painful gasps.

Cooper was in no better shape, his eyes glittering with unfulfilled passion, his body hardened from repressed desire.

With great effort he spoke.

"I promised myself I would take it easy," Cooper told her, his voice low and painfully raspy. "But I get within feet of you, and all the promises to myself and all my good intentions fly out of the window." Looking ruefully down at himself, he readjusted his jeans. "And my anatomy takes over and takes a beating."

L.J. stiffened. So it was only raw, unadulterated lust.

While, on one level, L.J. was pleased that she could inspire such passion in a man like Cooper, on a deeper, more compelling level, she was disappointed. Disappointed both on behalf of Cooper, whom she had thought had more depth and character than that, and for herself, since he seemed to follow the pattern of men she'd always encountered.

Knowing that for Mona's sake, as well as for herself, she'd better defuse the moment, L.J. said with an air of unconcern, "I know what you mean. I also told myself that chemistry was no excuse to become involved with anyone. Not only am I too busy at this juncture in my career to become seriously involved, but I really don't need any added complications."

"What about Dr. Gallagher?" Cooper could not resist asking. Did L.J. mean it? Had she only been carried away by passion—and nothing else? Yes, he'd been aroused, but there was a deeper level of involvement for him. Could she be so inure to him on an emotional level because Roarke Gallagher already held a special place in her heart?

L.J. stepped farther away from Cooper and put the lid on the cooler...and her own emotions.

"That, Mr. Channahon, is none of your business." Picking up the cooler, she indicated the two thermoses that she always had ready with hot chocolate and coffee in case anyone dropped by while she was working in the field. "If you'd be so kind as to bring those two with you, we can give Mona some help. She's bound to wonder how come the adults are taking such an extensive break."

Twelve

"Hey, what took you guys so long? Is this child-slave labor, like they had in old England? If so, I rebel," Mona protested, looking avidly from Cooper to L.J. and back again.

When she straightened, grabbing her back and moaning piteously, Cooper said, unmoved, "Well, it didn't take long to prove you can't take it. I guess anthropology is not the career for you after all."

"That has nothing to do with it," Mona denied hotly. "It's just that it's no fun working out here by myself, and with no one to ask if I'm doing the right thing. I'd hate to destroy some valuable evidence from the past."

L.J. moved over to Mona and gave her a quick hug. "Ignore your grumpy uncle. He's getting old. But you, my dear young lady, have the right instincts for an archaeologist, and from what I can see, you have *really* been working hard."

Mona blushed prettily from the compliment, and her eyes glowed. "See, Uncle Coop. I *am* the right woman for the job."

"Woman?" Mona's expression darkened again, and Cooper laughed. "Ah, you can dish it out, but you can't take it. First *you* were telling me I'm getting old, and now our esteemed doctor has jumped into the fray. My feelings are really hurt."

"Best thing for that is hard, physical labor," L.J. said, handing him some tools and delicate brushes. "After a quick lunch, you get to join in the fun."

Later that afternoon, Bradford Palmington arrived from Morton. It was a two-hour drive, but he'd only had a half day of classes because of teacher conferences.

L.J. was glad for the help. Bradford had participated in quite a few digs, and was being mentored by both herself and Roarke, as part of a central Illinois gifted young anthropologists program. With Bradford to keep an eye on Mona's progress, she could concentrate on Cooper's efforts.

And Cooper was really trying. He might not possess Mona's manual dexterity, touch and instinct for a find, but what he lacked in hand-eye coordination, he made up in sheer determination and extra care.

L.J. worked on a section of the dig that looked promising, but also took time to answer questions, and occasionally visited the other volunteers.

As she began digging around a tiny mound that indicated a small figurine might lay underneath, L.J. heard Mona's excited call.

"L.J.! I think I've got something!"

L.J. jumped to her feet. No matter how long she'd been working digs, the promise of a glimpse into the past thrilled her.

Carefully sprinting to Mona's side, L.J. saw the teenager painstakingly brushing some fragments of pottery.

Cooper and Bradford joined them, and L.J. took the pieces from Mona, who was shaking with anticipation.

"Wonderful, Mona!" L.J. said, smiling. "What do you think this is, Bradford?"

Bradford carefully, almost religiously, picked up the fragments from L.J. and said, his face beaming, "The design is that of a stylized bird. From their curved shape, I'd say they are part of a Hopewell bowl."

Cooper took one of the pieces in his broad palm and L.J. said, "Very good, Brad. Let's set them down in that foam-filled box. And let's see if there is more where that came from."

All of them, including Cooper, returned to their respective places with renewed vigor. Archaeologists did not expect to find outlandish treasures or mummy-filled tombs, but lived for the small revelations and views into history and culture that they could extrapolate from tiny remnants from the past.

Squatting down and suppressing a groan, Cooper looked over the site.

Mona was busy as a beaver, her quick, talented hands greedily sifting through dirt.

Bradford was similarly enthralled, his large frame—the boy had to be over six two, two hundred pounds—bent at an impossible angle over his portion of earth. His fair hair shone in the sun, and Cooper was at a loss to understand why Mona didn't like the kid. He was polite, a hard worker and totally dedicated to the same profession Mona loved.

L.J.'s voice cut into his reverie. "Did Roarke say when he was coming up, Bradford? I tried to reach him, but his beeper seemed to be off."

Bradford turned his head briefly to answer.

"I saw him last night when he tutored me in my independent studies paleontology class. Someone stole his beeper, his laptop and a case full of notes."

"Poor Roarke!" L.J. said, pausing to wipe some perspiration from her forehead. "Did he lose a lot of data?"

"He had some of it backed up on disk. He was

wondering if he could use your computer when he comes up next weekend.''

''Of course,'' L.J. said. ''I'll help in any way I can.''

Poor Roarke, my foot, Cooper thought as he forcefully stabbed around some rocks in the ground.

He snuck a look at L.J.'s pretzellike figure. He wondered if she'd been a gymnast, because her body seemed that of a contortionist as she twisted this way and that, and finally lay facedown on the dirt, trying to get a better view of the many-layered hole she'd so diligently sculpted.

In deference to the rising and unseasonal heat of the afternoon, L.J. was wearing khaki shorts and an open-necked vivid green blouse that made her eyes look like ripe limes.

Cooper realized that he seemed to be thinking of L.J. in terms of edible metaphors lately.

He was hungry for her…and not just for her body.

Cooper craved L.J.'s smile, her ready wit, her warmth and empathy.

He wondered if she felt as drawn to him.

Oh, he knew they both shared an undeniable chemistry. But Cooper wanted more than sex from L.J., and he'd not been able to figure out what L.J. expected from him.

L.J. had succumbed to their mutual sexual attraction—somewhat. But Cooper realized that L.J. was too secure a person, too strong a personality, that unless she felt more than a physical attraction for him, he was doomed. Particularly if "poor Roarke"—the wild card in this affair—already held the winning hand.

Shaking his head, Cooper returned to his work, telling himself that he'd better concentrate on the past, and leave the present for the near future.

After two more hours of digging, Cooper got up and tried to straighten his back.

It proved an arduous undertaking. Cooper's spine felt like it would never be the same, and he was convinced that he'd sport a dromedary's hump the rest of his life.

"Uncle Coop, are you all right!" Mona solicitously said, running to his side.

Cooper could have done without the attention.

"Yes, I'm fine, Mona. Just a bit thirsty."

"But you're *not* fine, Uncle Coop," Mona insisted, slipping an arm about his waist. "You look positively green around the gills."

"Really, Mona, I'm—"

"L.J., I think my uncle needs a rest," Mona called out.

L.J. pushed herself up with ease and hurried over to Cooper's side.

Cooper would gladly have strangled his niece.

"I wonder if this is how the precursors of Homo

Erectus looked," Mona mused aloud. "Sort of hunched over and—"

"Mona, I'm in a lot better shape than our predecessors," Cooper bit out.

"But you're not as young as you once were, Uncle Coop," Mona insisted. "You're starting to look sort of decrepit."

"Thank you for that vote of confidence, Mona," Cooper said wryly as he made another manly attempt at a vertical posture. His niece was making him feel about as youthful as the artifacts they were unearthing. "But I'm not feeble and infirm yet. And I'll have no trouble becoming…"

Frowning, aware of possible land mines, Cooper paused.

He noticed L.J.'s quickly hidden smile. "Getting erect? Oh, I'm convinced you won't."

Cooper would ordinarily have appreciated seeing the laughter in L.J.'s face, but not when it came at his own expense—especially after hearing Bradford's barely contained guffaw.

Mona's one-track mind concentrated on the problem at hand.

"Don't you think my uncle needs a rest, L.J.?" Still valiantly trying to prop a thoroughly vexed Cooper, Mona suggested, "And maybe some Ben-Gay?"

Cooper's ever-darkening expression penetrated Mona's tunnel vision, and she amended. "Or maybe some sports cream? Or how about the liniment Serena gave you? Perhaps he could rest on the couch for a while? If you help Uncle Coop get to the trailer, Bradford and I can finish out here.''

L.J., who was wincing inwardly at Cooper's obvious discomfort—both physical and mental—had to contain her mirth as he absorbed Mona's continued piling of unintentional insults.

"Uncle Coop is still ambulatory, thank you for your concern, dear niece,'' Cooper said through grinding teeth. ''I may look like a relic to you, but I've a while yet before I join the compost heap.''

It finally dawned on L.J. what Mona's ulterior motives were. With any other girl Mona's age, L.J. would have suspected that the teenager was trying to maneuver some time alone with Bradford. But Mona found the boy too dictatorial and had too much pride to chase after him.

No, Mona was after another romantic pairing.

Herself and Cooper.

She shouldn't feel bad at having taken so long to catch on, L.J. told herself. After all, Cooper had known Mona all her life, and he'd not stumbled onto her master plan.

But all of Mona's outrageous words and actions were beginning to fall in place.

L.J. decided to go along with Mona—it was almost time to quit for the day, anyhow, and this way she could please and accommodate everyone.

She could appease Mona's matchmaking instincts,

save both Cooper's pride and his poor lumbar vertebrae, and yet satisfy her own curiosity as to the figurine she'd been slowly uncovering.

"Cooper and I will take our finding to the trailer, Mona. You and Bradford gather all the tools and cover up the site in case it rains, after you finish extracting that small artifact in my grid."

Mona and Bradford leapt to their feet and took over L.J.'s spot.

She had a good idea of what the figurine would be, but wanted to reward the two kids for their hard work and dedication.

While she and Cooper began gathering the stuff to take back to the trailer to sort and catalogue, Cooper said softly, "That was nice of you."

Thinking Cooper was referring to her closing up shop for the day, L.J. said, "Oh, it was about quitting time anyway. We want to have some energy left for Saturday and Sunday, which promise to be hot, muggy days."

"That's not what I meant," Cooper told her. "It was nice to give up your find to the kids."

L.J. shrugged her shoulders dismissively. "I've had my share of discoveries. Those two kids deserve the joy of a nice find after all the hard work they put in."

Walking with L.J. in companionable silence, Cooper reflected that L.J. was a truly generous person.

But that generosity seemed to extend to everyone but him.

L.J. had proffered her compassion to Mona upon learning of her deep loss. She had taken Bradford under her wing, and her mentoring would mean a lot to the boy later on. And of course, Roarke could count on her every assistance.

But what about him? Cooper wondered. Just where did he fit into the picture? he asked himself for the hundredth time.

L.J. stole a glance at Cooper.

He really looked beat.

He obviously had not engaged in this kind of physical labor recently—if ever.

Yet he'd taken it like a trooper, abusing his spine and treating each infinitesimal, fragile find with careful hands that while large and powerful, were also patient and gentle.

L.J.'s thoughts strayed to those same hands which had not been too patient the other night.

But Cooper had known they did not have much time and privacy with Mona in the next room. He had quickly stolen a caress, and made the most of it.

What would it be like to have Cooper's hands on her body if and when they did have privacy? And all the time in the world?

The erotic picture her mind painted caused L.J. to stumble.

Without dropping the box he was carrying, Cooper still managed to get an arm around her waist and steady her.

Although he let go of her instantly, L.J. read the same awareness in Cooper's steamy gaze that was licking through her veins.

L.J. tore her gaze away, and picked up her pace.

But where did she think she was running to?

What refuge could she seek from her own traitorous emotions?

Thirteen

Cooper helped L.J. find some room for the boxes in her already-crowded trailer.

L.J. shook her head in disgust.

"I've got to find some more space. This is ridiculous. From the preliminary staking, I know I'm on to a rich site. We have definite tie-ins to Southern Illinois/St. Louis, to Hopewell and Cahokia cultures."

"But that's wonderful!" Cooper said. Noticing L.J.'s less-than-thrilled look, he said, "Isn't it?"

"It's highly unusual. Plus I found some evidence of Maya glyphs in a tiny fragment, and even a small piece of a stone from the warrior-empire of the Aztecs, depicting human sacrifice."

Cooper frowned. "Even I know that is *definitely* unlikely. Have you told the kids?"

L.J. stretched her back. "No, not yet," she said, shaking her head. "Some of the pieces look definitely planted, but if they are fake, they are good imitations. But it's not just up to me to decide, even if they are out of place stratigraphy-wise. We need a wealth of evidence, and findings in proper layers and with extensive dating, before any true correlations can be made. But whether there is Maya diffusion—or someone like the APs contaminated the site—there is still a lot of legitimate findings here, both Hopewell and Cahokia."

Dispiritedly, L.J. dropped onto the chair by her desk, also laden with all kinds of paraphernalia. She covered her face with hands grimy and full of tiny cuts.

"There needs to be a lengthy, extensive excavation, on a scale I've no funding for. I've got to talk to Roarke."

Roarke again, Cooper thought, mentally grinding his teeth.

But he shook off his jealousy, and concentrated on L.J. He would rather have her laugh at him continuously through life than to see her so dejected.

"Hey, those hands are gross, as Mona would say," Cooper told her as he took them tenderly into his own. "What do you say we wash them, indulge in an extra hot shower—and then I'll take us all out to dinner.''

L.J. stared at their interlaced fingers, and felt the sting of tears in her eyes. Kindness did that to her, and she didn't want Cooper to see the emotional facet of her character.

"You're right." She got up swiftly, tugging at her hands. "They are filthy. I'd better wash up.''

Cooper heard the gruffness in her tone and, while holding on to her hands with one of his, he cupped her chin with the other.

"You know, it's okay to show some human frailty. I know how much you care for your work. No shame in spilling a few frustrated tears. I've spilled some of my own while suffering through Wall Street caprice.''

L.J. very much doubted it, but she did like this side of Cooper. She enjoyed it too much, in fact, to allow his consoling to go much further.

They were as combustible as dry timber and a ready match. Tenderness could quickly turn into passion, and the kids were due in any minute.

"It's turning dark already, and I've got a lot to do yet. Do you mind if I take a rain check on it?''

"Tomorrow night, then? Dinner? You pick the time and place?''

L.J. nodded, her crying bout abating. Cooper was good for her.

But how long would he stick around? And knowing his possible power over her, how could she capitulate any of her hard-won freedom and peace of mind?

Her mother had enjoyed neither, and had perished of a broken heart, never thinking of the pieces she was leaving behind for an equally devastated daughter.

Those pieces had never quite been put together.

"Tomorrow night it is," Cooper said, smiling.

L.J. felt a frisson of fear sneak into her heart at the promise lacing Cooper's words.

The following day passed quickly and relatively uneventfully.

The two teenagers were buoyed by the various discoveries and worked harder, if possible.

Cooper, on the other hand, moved with considerable care. He had made use of Serena's liniment—L.J. had declined Cooper's request that she rub it into his sore back—and declared it magical. Although L.J. had told him he did not have to dig, that she could use his help on the analysis end, Cooper's male ego would not let him surrender so easily.

Nor would he enjoy volunteering so much if he were to do it away from L.J., his main reason for laboring at this hellish site in the first place.

The day turned cloudy, and L.J. called a halt a half hour earlier than the previous day.

"Do you think it's going to rain, L.J.?" Mona

asked. L.J. had painfully tried to disabuse Mona of her idolatry, but had not succeeded.

Short of being direct, and possibly hurting the girl's feelings, L.J. had no recourse.

But Bradford had no such compunction.

"What a question, Mona! As if L.J. would have the answer. You might think she's God, but she's no divinity. Not even a meteorologist."

Although quite impatient himself with Mona's attitude, Cooper thought Bradford's comment a bit cruel. He was about to intercede on his niece's behalf, when a well-placed elbow robbed him of both breath and speech.

"Oh, you're just saying that because you're a superior, sexist male chauvinist pig. *You* probably think you're God. You're certainly acting like it, lording it over a lowly freshman."

Cooper's defensive bristles retracted. He smiled down at L.J., silently thanking her for her opportune assault on his body.

Mona *was* able to take care of herself. To him, she'd always be the pink-cheeked, fuzzy-haired chubby baby that had held on to his finger shortly after birth, but had never let go of his heart.

Bradford looked affronted for a minute. He glared at Mona for a tense moment, before throwing back his head and laughing.

"You're a riot, kid. I bet you take no prisoners on a basketball court."

"Care to try me?" a bristly Mona challenged.

Bradford tapped the tip of Mona's dusty, upturned nose, and said, "You're on, kid. I mean, Mona."

"That's better," Mona said, getting a tarp to cover the section she'd been working on.

L.J. and Cooper exchanged amused glances, and Bradford told Mona, "And, hey... Listen, I'm sorry if I came on too—"

"Smug and hateful?" Mona sweetly supplied.

Bradford laughed again.

"I know I'm an exalted senior, half pint, but I didn't mean to hurt your feelings."

Bradford went back to his own spot, leaving Mona sputtering. "Half pint? I'll show that conceited, low-life, slimy—"

"I think he was teasing," Cooper told his niece, who looked like a candidate for apoplexy.

Mona considered her uncle's words for a minute. "Oh. It's okay, then. I guess."

"Lighten up, Monie. You don't want to have a heart attack before you reach Bradford's age, do you?"

"Oh, come on, Uncle Coop. I'm sure I'll get to *your* advanced age, at least."

"Ouch!" said Cooper, smiling as L.J. laughed at Mona's quick, sharp rejoinder.

Cooper and L.J. worked in unison to cover up the rest of their side of the dig, and he asked her, "Have you picked out the restaurant for tonight?"

Before L.J. could answer, Mona loped over. Cooper realized that his little niece was on the verge of disappearing, turning into a young lady overnight.

"Can I go out with Bradford instead of with you and L.J.? Bradford says after he showers and changes at the house he's staying at, he'll pick me up at the hotel. We can have a quick pick-up game at the local gym, and then we can take in a movie. They're showing a film I've been dying to see."

"Where *is* Bradford staying at?" Cooper asked, his expression a study of suspicion.

L.J. almost laughed out loud. Heaven help the little girl who became Cooper's daughter if he ever married and settled down with a family.

"Bradford has some family friends that put him up when he comes over to help me out. Quite respectable and trustworthy," L.J. assured him.

Cooper frowned at L.J. He obviously did not think she appreciated all the ramifications of Mona going out on a date.

Fortunately, L.J. was seeing a lot clearer than a concerned, overprotective uncle whose vision was hampered by a red veil.

"Can I, can I, Uncle Coop?" Mona said, almost jumping up and down in her excitement.

Bradford came over and told Cooper. "I'll have her back safe and sound."

The look Cooper threw Bradford promised dire

retribution if that were not the case. His unspoken message was: *You'd better, or else...*

"Have her back at the hotel by ten, then."

"Oh, Uncle Coop. The movie won't even start until seven. And we need time to play some basketball, and catch a bite to eat."

"You could come with us and have dinner, as we'd planned," Cooper reminded his turncoat niece.

Mona was certainly quick on her feet.

"But I'm not hungry enough for a fancy restaurant. I'd just like a hot dog, or a taco. Something quick and light." For added effect, she added, "I really need to practice some. My shooting will deteriorate from lack of work."

Cooper refrained from stating the obvious, that she could not cover two nests with one feathery rear.

He capitulated. "All right. Eleven."

While not totally happy, Mona was wise enough not to press it.

L.J. of course realized that Mona was trying to secure added time, not only for herself for a fun Saturday night out, but for what she obviously expected to be a grand seduction scene from Cooper.

Poor, deluded child.

But certainly single-minded about her goals.

"Thank you, Uncle Coop," Mona said, dropping a quick kiss on Cooper's cheek.

L.J. could almost see Cooper melting into a puddle right at her feet.

He was really helpless against his niece.

"Let's get this show on the road before we start tripping over each other in the dark," L.J. said, to give Cooper some time to recover.

Cooper's gaze went from Mona to Bradford, and back again, but he didn't say another word.

Within minutes, they were all on their way to the trailer.

Fourteen

"**D**o you want us to enter some of the field data, L.J.?" Mona asked as they all had lemonade and their choice of apple or pecan pie. Serena, who knew L.J. was expecting some company, had brought over a couple of her homemade beauties early that morning.

"Oh, that's sweet of you, Mona," L.J. said, savoring her bite of rich pecan pie. "But you need to start getting ready for your date."

"A date!" Mona exclaimed, outraged. "This is *not* a date. It's a challenge, and I'm going to rub Bradford's nose all over the court."

Bradford looked totally unconcerned, his gray eyes

intent on another piece of apple pie. L.J. gave him an extralarge portion, and Mona quickly finished her own piece, extending her plate for another slice. L.J., hiding a smile, served Mona an equally gargantuan portion.

"How about you, Cooper?"

"Thanks, L.J. But one piece is enough. Serena's a wonderful baker, but I'd like to save my appetite for dinner." Watching as his niece made short work of her pie, Cooper added pointedly, "Unlike someone I know who was not hungry and just wanted a *light* snack."

"Oh, this is something I don't get too often—homemade food, you know," Mona said, greedily eyeing a third slice. She looked at Bradford—whom she obviously did not want to get the upper hand in anything—to see if he were going to ask for another piece, and then at her uncle, whose piercing gaze was trained on her.

Obviously abandoning her plan of gluttony, Mona told L.J., "You know, it'd be a waste of time for Uncle Coop to take me to the hotel and then come back here to pick you up."

"Oh, I'm just going to take my car," L.J. said.

"No! I mean, that's a waste of gas and natural resources." Ignoring Cooper's raised eyebrows, Mona continued, "If you tell us what to do, we can help enter some things into the computer while you shower and get dressed. Then, Bradford can take me to the hotel, and while I take a shower and change, he can go over to the house and do the same. That way, once you're done, L.J., you can go over to the hotel and wait while Uncle Coop gets ready.''

"Boy, you should have been a general, getting the troops ready for battle with your complicated strategy," Bradford said.

Mona preened from the compliment, but Cooper was sifting through his niece's suggestion with a fine-tooth comb.

"And Brad would be waiting for you in *your* hotel room while you get ready?" Cooper asked.

"No, of course not," Mona said, impatiently looking at her watch. "That would be a waste of time. And the whole point of this is to have time to enjoy our Saturday. Bradford will be getting ready while I do, and then he'll come over to pick me up. His friends' house is close to the inn.''

L.J. could follow the inner workings of Mona's mind with no problem. Cooper's niece was trying to give *him* time to score, not her own date—or nondate, as Mona so ferociously maintained.

But Cooper was so focused on the possibility of a teenage boy's impulses getting the best of him—no doubt from personal experience, L.J. thought—that he could not conceive *his* own cunning teenager of trying to give him added time to get *his* date in a romantic mood.

"Anything funny?" Cooper asked L.J.

"Oh, come on, Uncle Coop!" Mona asked, her face a study of innocence, her big blue eyes wide enough to melt a glacier. "Don't you trust me?"

Of course, Mona, the little minx, had him there.

Cooper could not very well say aloud what was on his mind—that he did not trust Bradford.

And L.J., who knew the boy and trusted him implicitly, did not intend to make things easier for Cooper.

"Come on, Uncle Coop, get with the program here. Time stands still for no man."

"All right, all right," Cooper grumbled, still resistant to the plan, but finding no easy or polite way to oppose it.

"Well, L.J.?" Mona turned her sights on her. "What do you want us to do before you go get ready?"

The implication there was that L.J. should hop to it.

It never occurred to Mona that L.J. could be on to her scheme.

After all, what harm could there be in Mona's plan? L.J. knew Bradford would never harm a hair on Mona's Machiavellian head, and as for herself, she could very well take care of herself.

Not that Cooper would pose much of a problem. As they'd walked to the trailer, Cooper had looked less like Don Juan, than another fictional character, the Hunchback of Notre Dame.

Cooper's back would not allow him anything too strenuous, and he was unlikely to be thinking in terms of seduction.

"Okay, Mona. Thank you for the offer. You and Bradford come into my office and I'll tell you what to do."

L.J. realized an hour later that she had greatly underestimated Cooper.

His back *was* obviously bothering him. But his mind was suffering no such impediment.

When L.J. had emerged from her bedroom clad in a flowing dinner dress of green and gold, the colors shifting under the overhead illumination and heightening the copper highlights in her hair and the jade in her eyes, Cooper's gaze had slid admiringly and devouringly over her figure.

The big bad wolf had nothing on Cooper. He was eating her alive, right before witnesses.

L.J.'s witnesses, though, were too occupied having one of their frequent arguments.

And while the teenagers' bickering covered up the tension in the small trailer, once Mona had gotten into Bradford's old clunker there was nothing to defuse the sexual heat that Cooper radiated in his sports car.

"You look beautiful," Cooper told L.J. huskily once she was settled in his car.

"Thank you," L.J. said nervously.

Where was the confidence she had experienced only a short while ago? L.J. suddenly felt like a shy, awkward teen—and it had been a long time since she'd been that young and uncertain.

But there was no getting around the fact that Cooper and she shared a powerful attraction. Even now, with Cooper dusty, his hair a wild mess from the wind and dirt, she found him compelling.

His was a strong presence. He was too commanding to be ignored, and L.J.'s own response to him made the situation even more explosive.

L.J., needing to relieve some of the tension, asked the first thing that came into her mind.

"How come Mona's father doesn't bring her down here?"

"What, trying to get rid of me already?" Cooper asked, his amused glance traveling over her features from the glossy gold-brown waves that were held back at the nape in a mosaic barrette, to the straight nose, to the rounded but determined chin, and back up to the full lips that split in a reluctant smile.

When Cooper returned his gaze to the road, L.J. started breathing again, until his eyes sought the answer in her own startled green ones.

"No, of course not. I was just wondering how come your brother doesn't spend more time with his daughter."

"Corbett hasn't fully recovered from the loss of

Lauren. He adored his wife, and I'm afraid it's taken him longer to bounce back than it has Mona."

"One could attribute that to the natural resilience of youth," L.J. said thoughtfully. "But it could also be that Mona is not dealing with all her feelings, or is trying to hide them."

Cooper was silent for a moment. "You might have something there. Mona is *very* protective of her father. She could be trying to spare him grief by acting happier than she really is."

"Protectiveness runs in the family," L.J. said, smiling.

Cooper growled, having no trouble understanding her reference. "If Bradford even lays a hand on Mona—"

"Relax. Not only is Bradford a good kid, but you're underestimating your niece," L.J. said. Just as she had her uncle, she added silently.

"What about you? Are your parents supportive of your career choice?"

"No one was ever really supportive of my choosing anthropology," L.J. said casually, but Cooper sensed the hurt underneath. "My ex-fiancé used to say there was no money in it."

"The important thing is whether there is any satisfaction in it," Cooper said.

"Well, to Nick, lots of money and satisfaction were synonymous," L.J. said. "You should be able to relate to that. You've chosen a career that is highly remunerative.''

"But I also found satisfaction in it. I found it a challenge to outwit the market, try to predict the economy, outguess the opposition.''

"Found?''

"I'm afraid that in the past few years the glitter has dulled and the satisfaction has waned. In short, my career has become a job, and an unfulfilling one at that.''

L.J. reflected on Cooper's words. His statement truly set him apart from Nick, but she still felt that they were perhaps more alike than not.

"You obviously have no shortage of job satisfaction.'' Cooper cut into her thoughts. "But what about your parents? Surely they would want what would make their daughter happy? And your brothers or sisters?''

"I'm an only child,'' L.J. said. "And as for my father, he was a charmer, but a cheating one. He finally left one day when I was ten years old, breaking my mother's heart, and I haven't seen him since. My mother died a few years later. She never went on with her own life, because she'd expected my father to repent the error of his ways, and come back to her.''

"Maybe she was right,'' Cooper said gently. "Maybe she knew your father really loved her, and could one day kick his weakness.''

"Oh, I don't think it was a weakness at all," L.J. said, a bitter smile curving her lips. "I just think that monogamy is not that common in men. Nick certainly was not willing to stop straying."

Cooper felt a large piece of the puzzle fall into place.

For all of L.J.'s accomplishments and love of her work, the loves of her life had thoroughly disappointed her. And left her pretty much a cynic, unwilling to trust.

From what he'd seen of the male half of the human race, Cooper couldn't say he blamed her. But he knew one thing: the Channahon men—from his father to his three uncles, to his brother, Corbett—had been one-woman men.

Cooper had always shied away from commitment. But not because he thought himself incapable of fidelity, but because he'd seen his father heartbroken when his wife had died, as well as his oldest uncle, and own brother.

He'd been reluctant to make a commitment for fear of getting hurt.

But now he found he was even more deathly afraid of losing L.J. *before* they had a chance to have a go at a life together.

The question was: Was L.J. capable of loving? Would she let *him* into her heart? If that heart was not already given to someone else?

Fifteen

L.J. walked around Cooper's suite restlessly.

Mona had showered and changed into sweats in record time, somewhat reassuring her uncle with her casual attire and her renewed challenge of Brad's basketball prowess.

L.J. could read Uncle Coop's mind: he was hoping any physical activity would be confined to the basketball court.

Mona had kissed her uncle goodbye, and she and Brad—who had decided to wait while she got ready—had taken off in a cloud of boundless teenage energy and enthusiasm. Brad had further reassured Cooper before leaving that his mother's cousin, Mrs. Anderson, would be at the house.

L.J. had some energy left herself, but unfortunately it was the nervous kind.

With his briefcase open on the hotel desk, and papers neatly piled next to it—apparently he *was* busy at work, but had not wanted to deny Mona—and items of clothing strewn about the room, Cooper seemed ever present.

The shower went suddenly silent, and L.J. jumped.

She covered her heart with her hand, marveling at her agitation.

And yes, anticipation.

L.J. had been giving herself pep talks, much as a coach at halftime during a playoff game, but those talks had been falling on deaf ears.

That insidious temptress, rationalization, was beckoning to L.J.

What would be the harm of a "quick roll in the hay"?

After all, both she and Cooper were mature adults. It had been a long time since L.J. had been in a relationship that was not platonic—and she was a normal woman, with normal needs.

When the door flew open, L.J. had not made up her mind.

But she was very much afraid, from the gleam in Cooper's eyes, that he would do everything in his power to help her make it up to his satisfaction.

Her glance traversed Cooper's sleekly muscular, powerful frame.

Cooper had on only his slacks, and barefoot, with the belt of his trousers open, beads of water pearling on the glowing, tight skin, he emitted raw energy, pulsing male magnetism.

L.J. realized from the way Cooper's sensual, rather thin lips moved, that he had said something.

"I'm sorry?" L.J. asked, feeling the blush already staining her body turning an even darker hue.

Cooper was holding out something to her.

"Would you do the honors? A scalding hot shower helped, but I think I'd better do as my smart-alecky niece said, and put some ointment on my back so that I'm able to make it to the restaurant and back."

L.J. hesitated for a fraction of a second.

Cooper's extended hand seemed to mock her, challenge her.

Was she going to be less courageous than a mere slip of a girl?

Granted, Mona was not thinking of sex at the moment—at least, L.J. hoped to God she wasn't.

Cooper would never force her into anything, L.J. knew. He had not even taken a step toward her, apparently content to let her make all the moves.

All she had to fear was fear itself, L.J. told herself.

Yeah, right, the tiny bit of her mind that was still functioning on a logical level snorted.

L.J. put one foot in front of the other and approached Cooper.

Cooper could read several emotions flitting through L.J.'s face.

He saw passion, fear, desire, longing, caution, and ultimately, some sort of decision.

Only, he could not read which way L.J. had decided.

But he could not make up L.J.'s mind for her. Yes, he was more than willing to show her how much he wanted her, and even entice her into making love with him.

But L.J. had to come to that decision of her own accord.

He was willing to extend the apple, but she had to walk freely to take it from his hand and bite into it.

L.J. reached Cooper and took the tube from his hand.

It wasn't Ben-Gay, she noted, but some highly touted sports cream.

Cooper noticed L.J. studying the brand.

"I'd already decided I was going to need some external help in surviving your life's work, so I decided to buy some items at the local pharmacy last night. I already finished Serena's magical potion."

L.J.'s gaze flew to his. She wondered what other items he might have picked up, but she did not dare ask.

Cooper, a rueful smile on his face, added, "As you can see, it is a famous brand name supposedly favored by highly trained and coordinated athletes. I guess the rest of us mere mortals are supposed to identify with those supremely skilled, outrageously salaried jocks.''

L.J. smiled back.

"Well, let's see if it helps."

Cooper turned to the bed, and carefully lay on it after unzipping his slacks and pulling them down to the middle of his buttocks.

L.J. saw he was not wearing any underwear, and swallowed past the avaricious lump in her throat.

Gingerly, she sat next to Cooper, and almost jumped off the bed when his voice, half-muffled as his face rested on a pillow, asked, "Do you think you could massage my back a little? I think it would help relax my muscles."

But not mine, L.J. thought, as indeed, hers tightened, and a curl of awareness blossomed deep within her.

She set down the tube of cream and put her hands on Cooper's back.

"Unless your arms are ten feet long, I think you'd better get closer," Cooper said, his voice suspiciously off-key.

Was he laughing at her?

L.J. moved closer on the bed and flexed her fingers. Nick had said she had digits of steel, and Cooper would get what he asked for: a thorough massage.

She began with deceptive mildness. Her fingers

merely touched the warm, smooth male skin, fleetingly, from shoulders to waist.

"A bit harder, please," Cooper asked.

L.J.'s grin was evil.

After one more gossamer trip over Cooper's strong, beautiful back, L.J. began in earnest.

At first, Cooper groaned with satisfaction. He stretched like a cat, arching his back cautiously.

But soon, he seemed to be retreating into the mattress like a turtle into its shell.

"Ah, that's okay, I think—L.J.," Cooper gasped, but this time it was not from delight. "We'd better get going, or we'll be late for dinner."

"Oh, no rush," L.J. said, hitting his back with the edge of her palms. "No need for reservations, and I think you need a bit more loosening up."

She proceeded to give it to Cooper, who bit off another groan.

Then, when he seemed limp on the bed, L.J. added the cream—slowly, sensually.

Cooper groaned once more, especially as L.J.'s fingers neared his waist and slipped below it.

L.J. didn't stay in that nether region too long.

Those sinfully curved buns looked too luscious, as did the small waist that opened up into a broad chest and wide shoulders.

Rubbing the cream in thoroughly, L.J. bolted from the bed and into the bathroom, ostensibly to wash her hands.

"You'd better put on a shirt right away," L.J. advised. "You have to keep your back warm."

An indistinct sound emerged from the bedroom, and L.J. stayed in the bathroom long enough to give Cooper time to dress.

When she emerged, the sight of him took her breath away.

The dark blue suit, with light blue shirt, deepened the ocean hue of his gaze and made his shoulders seem even wider.

Both of them stood there, each feasting on the other's face and body, yet reluctant to make the first move.

Finally Cooper got out a low, strangled word. "Ready?"

Was she ever!

But she supposed he meant for dinner.

Wishing she could erase the past, dispense with her doubts and fears, her distrust and hard-won caution, L.J. nodded wordlessly.

Cooper saw the indecision in L.J. He could almost taste her desire, and had a pretty good idea she wanted him almost as much as he wanted her.

But L.J. was nothing if not self-controlled.

And because she'd shared some of her pain and anguish with him, Cooper did not want to take advantage of her in such an obvious place.

It smacked too much of propinquity. And although

one side of Cooper wanted L.J. any way he could have her, another, more thoughtful side, wanted to make sure that when he made love to her, that it would be because she wanted *him* and was not carried away by mere passion.

There was nothing wrong with passion between consenting adults, but L.J. had come to signify a lot more to him than scratching an itch.

Cooper walked over to the chair where L.J. had draped her coat. Picking it up, he waited as she slowly moved over to him.

He held it in place for her, and as she slipped her arms into the sleeves, he leaned into her.

His hands rubbed her arms gently over the wool material and slid upward to her neck, which he massaged slowly, softly.

L.J. leaned back into Cooper's warm, solid strength, an inarticulate murmur escaping her throat.

The needy sound of it shocked her and opened languid eyes that had closed at Cooper's tender caress. L.J. moved away from him and toward the door.

Cooper picked up his own coat, the hotel key, and followed L.J.

But as he was opening the door for her, the telephone rang.

Cooper frowned, and L.J. could once again read his mind.

Had something happened to Mona?

Striding toward the phone, Cooper picked it up and barked into it.

"Cooper Channahon."

The voice on the other end must have reassured him, because Cooper's stance lost its rigor mortis quality.

"We were just about to leave for dinner, Mona."

He listened for a moment, and his body stiffened again.

"No! You may not sleep over at Bradford's cousin's place. I want you back at eleven."

L.J. smiled. No wonder Corbett had not been able to deal with both Lauren's death and his strong-willed child. Mona was truly a handful.

"We have more than enough time to have a leisurely dinner, Mona. There are not too many places to go to afterward in this rural area. As soon as you get off the phone, we'll be able to get something to eat."

Cooper passed a weary hand over his face, and then raked his fingers through his dark wavy hair, tousling it even more sexily.

L.J. took the opportunity to enjoy her view of a truly gorgeous, compelling male, while Cooper matched wits with his sly niece.

"Eleven o'clock, Mona. Or L.J. will be left without one volunteer as of tomorrow."

That apparently did the trick, for Cooper was able to get off the phone right away.

He hung up forcefully, and endearingly raked his hair once more.

"I bet you didn't know what you were letting yourself into when you got involved with two Channahon volunteers," Cooper said, shrugging into his coat. "We must be more trouble than we're worth."

"Well, considering that volunteers are not knocking down my door in droves, I've got to take what I can get. Even were they subpar."

Cooper's gaze flew to hers guiltily, and L.J. added, laughingly, "Which these volunteers are not."

Cooper's coat collar was tangled, and she went up to him, telling him so. "Let me fix it."

As her arms went to his neck, smoothing both the shirt and coat collars, L.J.'s own coat gaped open, and her chest came into close contact with Cooper's.

Cooper's body resumed its previous rigidity, but for a very different reason. However, he didn't try to take her into his arms.

L.J. froze, her gaze locked with Cooper's.

Sixteen

For an instant...or an eternity...neither moved.

Cooper waited for L.J. to step away, but she could not have moved to save her life.

Slowly, very slowly, Cooper lowered his head.

His mouth touched briefly, fleetingly, against hers.

Slipping his thumbs under her chin to gently but firmly tilt her head, Cooper asked, "Are you sure you want this? It was not my idea to lure you into my lair, so to speak."

"I know," L.J. told him in a voice raspy with desire. "It was your niece's idea."

Cooper frowned. "Mona's? Why would she want me here, with you?" Anger darkened his gaze. "If she's thinking of making out with that boy—"

"Relax," L.J. told him, covering his mouth with her index finger. "I think she wants *us* to get together."

Cooper was apparently not thinking clearly at this moment, and L.J. couldn't blame him. Her thought processes could hardly be called analytical right now.

"Well, I can't say, whatever her motives, that her idea lacked merit."

Capturing her finger between his teeth, Cooper bit gently into it and then pulled it into his mouth, where he sucked at it.

A shiver went through L.J. He released her finger, and his hand went to the nape of her neck, pulling her face close to his. He spoke against her lips, his breath, his nearness, clouding her judgment. "Stop me if you don't want this."

The vibration of his words against her mouth was oddly erotic, and when he opened his mouth and then closed it over hers, her lips opened of their own accord.

L.J. felt herself floating, escaping herself and all rational thought. When Cooper's tongue invaded her mouth, she felt an echo in her loins. When he swept her tongue with his, exploring every secret, moist passage of her mouth, and then pulled on her tongue, L.J. whimpered.

Between her thighs, she also felt a pulling ache, an empty hollow, a waiting to receive.

Suddenly ravenous, L.J.'s hands threaded through

Cooper's silky hair, and she hungrily sought his tongue, engaging it in a desperate duel.

Cooper's hands went to her coat, and he swiftly pulled it off her shoulders. L.J. followed suit, divesting Cooper of his coat, and then starting on his shirt.

Suddenly their clothes were an offensive impediment.

With trembling fingers, they dispensed of jacket and shirt, dress and chemise.

Their lips connected here and there, as the clothes flew and were discarded on the floor.

L.J. was consumed by desire.

The flames were growing, a spreading conflagration that demanded to be put out.

Cooper stepped out of his slacks, and L.J. saw that he had not bothered to add underwear.

His manhood sprang proudly from a dark, curly thicket, and L.J.'s hands enclosed it, stroking it slowly, maddeningly.

Cooper dropped to his knees and jerked down her panties in one smooth motion. His hands closed over her breasts, squeezing them hard, enjoying their full luxuriance. When she moaned softly, he flicked and then pinched her nipples, holding them between thumb and forefinger, rolling them, and elongating them into tumescent passion. Overcome, L.J. rested her hands on Cooper's shoulders, adrift in a weightless world, floating outside herself.

Cooper kissed her stomach, and his tongue dipped inside her navel. A whimper escaped L.J. and she dug her fingernails into his back as his mouth descended ever lower, his lips nipping, his tongue laving, until he found that aching, waiting core.

L.J. was shivering now, her legs barely able to sustain her. Still holding on to the only solid entity in her drifting universe, Cooper's broad shoulder, she managed to bring her other hand to the front, and her own fingernail rasped against a male nipple.

Cooper gasped against her soft, brown curls, and he brought his hands down from her throbbing breasts to tenderly part her flesh, his fingers exploring just inside the velvety folds of her body.

L.J. bit her lower lip as one finger entered her, and unerringly went to the ultrasensitive, small nub, rubbing gently, skillfully.

Feeling her knees buckle, L.J. rested her weight on Cooper's broad shoulders. Blindly, desperately, she massaged the taut muscles and tried to pull away from the agonizing stimuli; at the same time her hips began a circling, rhythmic motion.

Cooper's long finger entered her fully, and he stroked her firmly, insistently. L.J. gasped, and she enclosed him as waves of heat erupted within her, starting to erase that hollow sensation deep in her womb. Her lower body tilted toward the source of the pleasure, and Cooper added another finger to his sensual play, massaging even deeper and harder.

L.J. couldn't take any more. She dropped to her knees, and Cooper withdrew his fingers, his hands going to her derriere to support her. Pulling her legs apart, Cooper sat her on his lap while he rummaged behind him, getting something from the pocket of his slacks.

Feeling suspended in air, her arousal intense but unfulfilled, L.J. licked Cooper's neck and bit it.

Cooper growled, and when he was done with the condom, lifted his hips.

L.J. slowly lowered herself onto him, feeling the throbbing, fiery length of his manhood driving into her, opening her, filling the painful void, deeply and consummately.

His pulsing shaft, embedding itself time and again into L.J., brought her quickly to the edge. Cooper's hands gripped her buttocks and massaged them, guiding her as she wrapped herself around him, the lower part of her body assuming a lone identity, heavy, ever tightening.

One more lunge, and she had crossed the threshold of pain and ecstasy, her inner contractions guiding him even deeper within her. The sizzling pleasure was such that L.J. did not even notice when Cooper ceased thrusting, content to hold her in his arms, his lips closing about one nipple, then the other, adding to the sensory assault that robbed her of reason and sanity.

Throwing her head back, L.J. cried out as one last,

powerful wave seized her, invading her body and leaving her spent and breathless.

Cooper held on to her, his hands gentling her, his touch caressing and reassuring.

L.J. lowered her head to his and kissed him, her tongue licking his lips, her teeth nibbling on his chin, and traveling lower to his neck.

L.J. could feel his tumescent shaft still embedded within her. She moved her hips slowly, experimentally, even as her mouth played upon his flesh.

Cooper groaned, his self-control almost gone, and he lifted her from his lap and laid her on the floor.

Grabbing his coat and spreading it on the rug, Cooper repositioned her, his passion-rigid body covering hers.

L.J. raised her knees, opening wide to accommodate him, her fingers raking his back and then settling on the taut buttocks.

Cooper swelled even more within her, and his hips charged into hers, driving her into the floor as he sought his own release.

Near the summit, his mouth sought hers, and he duplicated the mating below, his tongue delving deep within the hot moistness of her mouth, while his jolting thrusts brought L.J. once more to the summit.

Her second climax coincided with Cooper's, and it was wilder and even more satisfying.

He cried out her name as he spilled into her, and L.J. received his tongue as she shudderingly received him, feeling first alone, shattering into a thousand pieces, only to be made whole as they came together.

A deep shivering coursed through L.J.'s body as she clung to Cooper, and he folded her into his arms. Then Cooper got up, tenderly picked her up and carried her to bed.

He covered them with a blanket, but within minutes, the heat of passion had warmed her again, and L.J.'s lassitude disappeared into a sea of churning, sizzling sensation.

Cooper moved away long enough to look at the watch on the night table.

"Almost ten o'clock," he announced sorrowfully. "Are you hungry?"

L.J.'s stomach rumbled in answer, and she laughed. Cooper's broad palm covered her belly and gently massaged it.

"I think we'd better get dressed," L.J. said, regret evident in her voice. "Mona is quite unpredictable, and if she happens to get mad at Bradford, and asks him to bring her back early..."

Cooper nodded, and reluctantly got out of bed.

"Amazing what a little cream and a savage massage will do for one's back," Cooper told L.J. as he went to retrieve their clothes, still haphazardly lying on the carpet.

L.J.'s gaze followed him. He was unconcerned

with his nudity—not that he had anything to be concerned about, L.J. admitted.

"How about a quick shower first?" Cooper suggested as he dropped the clothes onto the bed.

"A very quick one," agreed L.J.

Before dropping her off, Cooper went through the Mexican drive-thru, and L.J. and Cooper engaged in a guilty pleasure: tacos, burritos and nachos, everything smothered in sour cream and cheese and peppers hot enough to burn the roof of one's mouth.

After a quick goodbye at L.J.'s trailer door, Cooper ran to his car. He wanted to be back before Mona, to ensure that his niece did not have to walk into a dark hotel room—and to make sure that she really did keep her curfew.

Promptly at eleven o'clock, Mona turned her key in the lock.

Cooper had business papers spread all over the couch, and when he looked up, a welcoming smile on his face, he felt it fading.

Mona was sporting a heavy frown.

"What happened, Monie? Bradford get out of line?"

"Bradford?" Mona said blankly. "Oh, Uncle Coop, you're so lame. I can handle Bradford. But what happened to L.J.? Didn't you guys go to dinner?"

"Yes, we ate," Cooper temporized. "And to answer the next question in your interrogation, L.J.'s back in her trailer. She's working tomorrow, you know. And so are we.''

"Oh," Mona said.

Cooper didn't like the sound of that.

"I'm supposed to be doing the questioning here, Mona. What's wrong? Are you too tired? Don't you feel well? If you'd like, we can go back tomorrow so you can have some time to rest and do your home-work—''

"No! Thanks, Uncle Coop, but I'm fine. Just a bit pooped. And I can handle the homework. I certainly don't want to disappoint L.J., who's counting on us.''

Going toward her bedroom, Mona asked Cooper over her shoulder, "Everything cool with L.J.? You guys didn't have a fight, did you?''

"A fight? Why would you think that?''

"Because when you two first met, you didn't make a first great impression, uncle dear,'' Mona said condescendingly, in that long-suffering way teenagers universally adapt. "Your comments didn't go over too well, the ones about anthropology, and romance novels—''

"And who was the one who repeated them to L.J.?'' Cooper reminded his niece.

Mona waved that insignificant detail aside, and came back into the sitting room.

"Don't stay up too late with those business files. Don't forget we're going over to L.J.'s site at eight.''

"As if I could forget." Cooper curiously looked on as his niece rummaged through her capacious purse and extracted a few paperback books.

"Here. Bradford took me to the local bookstore. These are used, but they'll do."

Cooper looked at the books Mona brought over. "Romances?"

"Yeah. L.J. and I were talking about who her favorite romance authors are. I wish I could have gotten a better selection—"

"Oh, I'm sure these are fine," Cooper said faintly.

"—but I don't get enough allowance money," Mona said pointedly. "So I was reduced to visiting the used bookstore, and these were the only ones I could get. They're pretty good, though."

"I'm sure they are," Cooper repeated. Handling the books gingerly, a perplexed look on his face, he asked of his niece, "What exactly do you expect me to do with these?"

"Why, read them, silly," Mona told her uncle, rolling her eyes. "What else?"

With that pronouncement, Mona made her way into the bedroom and left her uncle staring bewilderingly at the romance novels that were burning holes into his hands.

Seventeen

"Uncle Coop," Mona asked Cooper the following morning on their drive over to L.J.'s site. "What did you think of those romance novels I gave you?"

"'Fraid I haven't read them yet," Cooper said, stifling a yawn. The few muscles and tendons that the digging had not pulled or strained, his lengthy and acrobatic lovemaking with L.J. had.

Cooper felt that the phrase "sore all over" had been coined with just him in mind.

"Well, when are you going to?" Mona demanded impatiently.

Cooper could not hide another yawn, and his niece snorted inelegantly.

"Oh, great! You *are* turning into a fuddy-duddy," Mona said. "I wonder what L.J.'s going to think when she sees you can't even keep awake."

Cooper hid a grin. "She's going to think that I'm a very nice uncle, whose patience is being sorely tried after staying up until four in the morning, working on business papers, trying to catch up on his work, because he was foolish enough to give in to an ingrate of a niece's wheedling and whining."

"I don't whine," Mona said, affronted.

Cooper laughed, and found that even that small effort hurt.

"Ah, here we are," Cooper said, parking in his usual spot.

Mona grabbed the bag of fresh-baked goodies he'd picked up at the local bakery, and ran to the trailer.

L.J. opened the door and came out, carrying a leather case and a portable phone.

"A cellular?" Cooper asked. "Anything the matter?"

L.J. nodded. "The flooding is serious, down by Kampsville. They're afraid it might be worse than the one in '93."

"Surely you're not thinking of going, then?" Cooper asked. "It's bound to be dangerous."

"Roarke needs my help," L.J. said simply. "Bradford's coming with me, and we're going to try to salvage some of Roarke's work. The CAA's still underwater, and this is not going to help."

"CAA?" asked Cooper, frowning.

"Center for American Archaeology," L.J. reminded Cooper. "Are you coming?"

"L.J., you've got to reconsider this. You can't take a chance like this. And Bradford—I'm sure his parents would not like him to—"

"Bradford's parents already know, and they've given their permission. I'm on my way to pick him up now. I was just waiting in case you wanted to come along."

L.J. looked at Cooper, awaiting his decision.

"I'm sorry, L.J.," Cooper said, feeling a hot shaft of jealousy piercing his body. "I think you're wrong in running just because Roarke snapped his fingers."

"Of all the—" L.J. bit back her words with difficulty. "I'm not jumping just because Roarke says jump. He needs me, yes, but we have to salvage our heritage, the evidence from the past."

"I have to think of Mona," Cooper began stubbornly.

Mona was listening avidly to the exchange between the two adults. "I'd like to go, Uncle Coop. I'm sure—"

"Stay out of this, Mona," Cooper snapped. His niece, hurt by his tone and dictatorial attitude, curled her lower lip and shot visual daggers at her favorite uncle.

"This is *not* about Mona, and you know it," L.J. said. "I guess you still haven't changed your mind

about anthropology and moldy things, have you?"
Walking over to her car, L.J. threw over her shoulder,
"You are no different than Nick."

On the long way home, with an angry, silent Mona
by his side, Cooper had time to reconsider what L.J.
had said.

He still felt hurt that she'd contacted Bradford
right away, and he'd only learned of the crisis upon
arriving at the site.

But then again, Roarke's call had come in only an
hour before, and L.J. had been expecting them anyway.

But she could not very well have expected him to
drop everything. He had a job, after all, one he had
been neglecting lately, to please Mona and help L.J.
out.

L.J. was right. Although Cooper knew he'd made
the right decision in not endangering Mona, he also
knew he could have taken his niece home and come
back.

It would have been a long ride, but one he'd gladly
have made had it been L.J.'s site that had been under
danger of flooding.

But as soon as he'd heard Roarke's name, Cooper
had seen red.

Or green. Jealousy had reared its ugly head, and
it had jeopardized his burgeoning relationship with
L.J.

How stupid could one man be?

During the rest of the week, Cooper had plenty of time to ask himself that question.

But by the end of the work week, he had come to a conclusion.

Mona's relentless prodding and nasty accusations had played a part, too.

But Cooper had realized that Mona was right in some things. L.J. needed help, both with workers and financing, yet she'd not hesitated to go to the aid of a friend.

Cooper should have been secure enough to know that L.J. would not have responded as she had to him if she were in love with Roarke Gallagher.

But hindsight always produced twenty-twenty vision.

Cooper had a plan for L.J.'s site.

And more importantly, he had a plan for L.J.

And this time, Mona was *not* going to be involved.

In one of their many arguments, Cooper had confronted Mona about her constant interference, and she had confessed to trying to engineer the romance between L.J. and him.

Cooper recalled what L.J. had said, and how he had dismissed it in the heat of passion, and was embarrassed that a relative stranger had caught on to his niece's matchmaking scheme before he had.

But like he'd said before...females. They'd be the death of him yet, Cooper told himself, remembering

L.J.'s smooth, supple body and abandoned lovemaking. But what a death!

L.J. had time to reflect on her actions while she was down in southern Illinois.

Bradford had stayed until Monday, and L.J. had remained until Tuesday to give Roarke a hand.

They'd been able to salvage a lot of artifacts, data and findings, and for that, L.J. was glad.

Roarke returned with her, and spent the rest of the week alternately helping her at the site and borrowing her computer for his own work before leaving again Friday evening. His deadline loomed near, and Roarke felt that he had gone through every delay imaginable, and that Murphy's Law, in his case, must surely cease to exist.

Or at least ignore him for a year or two.

Serena dropped over, but her company and wonderful pies did not manage to cheer L.J. L.J. recognized that Cooper was right in being concerned about his niece, but he could have returned.

At the very least, he could have called.

Sighing, L.J. returned to her digging. She'd been right when she'd said Cooper had no respect for her career and life's work, and that he was no different than Nick.

Cooper was afraid to make a commitment.

When both Friday and Saturday came and went, L.J. had given up on Cooper.

And Mona.

L.J. found that she missed both Channahons, and realized that she'd have been glad to have been part of their obviously loving, close-knit circle.

One of the reasons that L.J. had taken the plunge and become involved with Cooper had been the warm affection and care he had shown for his niece.

But although Cooper might be crazy about his niece, the same could not be said about his feelings for her.

Saturday afternoon, L.J. decided to call it quits early. She was bone tired, and feeling quite depressed. After taking a shower, she was planning on going into town, and taking in a movie.

But as L.J. was ready to get into her car, she heard some screaming and swearing.

She turned around to see two APs—two very inebriated APs—approach her.

"Hey, grave digger. Want some company?" the taller of the two intruders asked, his voice thick and muddled.

L.J. shook her head, and felt for the keys in her purse.

"No, thank you. I'm ready to go into town."

"Well, that's okay, too. We'll accompany you," the shorter man said.

"I don't need any company," L.J. said, her hands finally closing about the large key ring. If need be, she could use it as a weapon.

"Aren't we uppity," the tall, balding man said with a sneer. "Way we hear it, you came here early, in late March instead of May, to protect your crummy bones and broken vases from us."

"Us!" the smaller man repeated, stabbing his chest with one dirty, broken fingernail.

Although fed up with the pair's aspersions on her site and its contents, L.J. chose to let the comments pass. The two men were drunk, and possibly dangerous.

"I'm sorry you feel that way. But just as you have to protect your camp from intruders, and safeguard your important discoveries, so do I."

"You got *that* right, sister," the short man said. "*We* have important disc—des—stuff," he concluded. "But *you* don't," he emphasized, pointing his finger at L.J.

"All right, I don't," L.J. said, turning quickly and inserting the key in the lock.

But before she could open the door, the taller man was upon her and had laid one beefy hand on the door.

"Where are you going in such a hurry? Don't you like our company?"

The man's breath almost keeled L.J. over. She strove to hide her fear, and said calmly, "I really have to go. Perhaps we can discuss this at another time over coffee."

"Are you saying that I'm drunk?" the AP said.

Moving closer to L.J., he smirked. "Well, let me show you I don't need no stinking cup of coffee to function. I'll—"

"You'll take your stinking self, and your partner here, and hightail it out of Dr. Livingston's site," another male voice said.

L.J., so intent on defusing the situation, and trying to make her getaway, had not even realized another car had driven up.

Cooper's presence only a few feet away was a welcome, reassuring sight.

"Move away from him, L.J.," Cooper said.

"No, you don't," the large man said, grabbing L.J.'s arm.

Reacting instinctively, L.J. slammed her keys into the man's bridge, and his nose started bleeding. When he still didn't release her, she raised her knee and slammed it into the man's groin.

This time he not only let her go, but dropped to his knees.

His companion jumped Cooper from behind, but Cooper made short work of the other man. Within seconds, the second drunk lay sprawled facedown in the dirt.

"New volunteers?" Cooper asked.

Eighteen

"**I**'m sorry about those two," Serena profusely apologized to L.J., who had called Serena and related what had happened. Serena had rushed right over.

"Don't worry about it," L.J. said, hugging her friend. "I know you had nothing to do with it."

"No, I didn't, but sometimes some radical elements sneak in. In this case, these two have less to do with paranormal than abnormal."

"Will they stay in jail long?" Serena asked the two policemen that had accompanied L.J. and Cooper over to AP headquarters.

"No, I'm sure they'll make bail. So Dr. Livingston here better be careful."

"Oh, I'm sure it'll be all right," L.J. said. "After all, they've been at Serena's camp for a few days, and they hadn't tried anything before today."

"Still, you'd better take precautions," Cooper said.

"They won't be members of the APs any longer," Serena promised. "They were part of Gordon Eppeinstein's group—the codirector of this convention and subsequent field study—but he's no longer codirector. I've put in for a permanent site, and will be waiting to see if it is approved."

"That's all we need," one of the policemen grumbled. "Past nuts in one field, future nuts in the other."

"I suggest you take care how you address Dr. Livingston," Cooper said, putting his arm about L.J.'s shoulder. "Anthropologists are not nuts."

"I noticed that you didn't include Serena Troy and her paranormals in your defense," the other officer said, amused. "Could it be you don't believe in aliens, Mr. Channahon?"

"Let's just say I prefer to reserve judgment," Cooper retorted.

His evasiveness did not fool either officer, and they both got a good belly laugh out of his answer.

"Well, gentlemen, if you don't mind, I'd like to get to bed," Serena said. "It's almost midnight, and I still have a lot to do."

"That's right. You people come out at night, don't you?" the rude officer said.

"Let's just hope the aliens don't decide to take you into one of their spaceships and conduct their experiments on you," Serena told him.

That set the two lawmen laughing again, and they left, shaking their heads.

"Narrow-minded cretins," Serena said, closing her fists in frustration.

"Hey, ignore it. I was called a grave robber by one of your esteemed APs," L.J. said, trying to make light of the situation.

"Ex-APs," Serena reminded L.J. "And you possess recognized credentials, and still command respect in most circles, while we are ridiculed and even attacked at every turn. Not excusing those two lowlifes that accosted you, but sometimes, I guess, some of my members just react out of sheer frustration."

"Well, neither of them better try to act out his frustrations anywhere near L.J.'s site, or I'll beat the crap out of them."

Why don't you take a shower?" Cooper suggested when he and L.J. had returned to her trailer.

"All right," L.J. agreed, suddenly feeling exhausted. Now that the adrenaline rush was over, her whole body seemed numb.

L.J. went to her bedroom to get a nightgown and robe before heading for the bathroom.

She saw Cooper setting a large duffel bag on the kitchen counter and asked, "Are you hungry? I could fix us an omelette—"

"Just go and take a nice, relaxing shower," Cooper said. "I brought some food with me, most of it already prepared or half-done."

L.J. emerged from a long, hot soak in the combination tub/shower feeling refreshed and surprisingly hungry.

She opened the bathroom door and halted in her tracks.

All the lights in the trailer were off, and everywhere she looked she saw candles.

They were flickering madly, since in such a small, enclosed space, they were emitting a rather unpleasant odor, and Cooper had been forced to open a couple of windows.

Come to think of it, L.J. had never recalled candles that smelled quite as rancid as these.

Cooper turned as she walked into the kitchen, and L.J. noticed there were still—unfortunately—more candles on the table. Apparently, another trait they possessed was that of giving off intense heat.

The delicate chocolate soufflé Cooper had procured from somewhere was diligently melting into an unseemly puddle, its previous elegance no longer visible.

"Please, sit down," Cooper asked.

L.J. sat. Her legs were no longer supporting her, in any case.

Off to one side, L.J. saw several dozen roses, of every imaginable hue. Their scent, normally so refreshing and evocative, blended with the stench from the candles to become sickeningly cloying.

But wait!

There was still another pungent aroma begging to be identified.

L.J. followed her nose, and noted caviar, oysters and shrimp on another section of her kitchen counter.

With a flourish, Cooper produced a box of Godiva chocolates.

Cooper could not possibly know it, but as a child, L.J. had OD'd on them. She'd eaten so many of them, she'd gotten thoroughly sick, and had never touched another one in her life.

Just the sight of them made L.J. queasy.

As a pièce de résistance, Cooper produced a bottle of fine champagne.

Cooper attempted to open it, but the stubborn bottle would not cooperate, so he desisted in his efforts and set it on the table before sitting next to her.

Overwhelmed, L.J. had kept silent throughout the entire proceedings.

"I bet you're wondering what this is all about," Cooper told her.

L.J. nodded. She was literally speechless, especially when she noticed Cooper's attire.

While she'd bathed, he'd changed into a buccaneer shirt, with long, flowing sleeves, and a high collar. He unobtrusively tried to open the neckline, but it, like the champagne, proved uncooperative.

Poor Cooper was sweating bullets.

Literally.

A meat-and-vegetable mousse, occupying the place of honor on L.J.'s small table, began to drip all over her lace hand-embroidered tablecloth, the mold losing its shape, the gelatin joining the already-darkening mass of the soufflé that had also over-flowed its elegant crystal dish.

"Well, I wanted to apologize for leaving you in the lurch last week. After taking Mona back, I could have returned and gone down to help you and Roarke."

L.J. nodded, unable to give Cooper her undivided attention because another smell had been added to the equation.

"Are you making something in the oven?" L.J. asked.

"Yes, thank you," Cooper said, jumping to his feet and almost knocking the table over.

L.J. lunged and grabbed at the various dishes in imminent danger of crashing to the floor.

Cooper came back, carrying in his hand a pan full of biscuits—blackened ones.

"I forgot to take them out in time," he said.

Once again he attempted to undo the high neck of

his pirate attire, but desisted as he continued his apology.

"I guess I was jealous of Roarke, and let it cloud my judgment. But I think *you* owe me an apology for comparing me to Nick. I'm nothing like that lousy—"

Whatever Cooper had been about to say was drowned by a loud pop, followed by a torrent of fuzz.

Cooper grabbed at the bottle, but the foaming, bubbly substance made the container slippery, and it fell into Cooper's lap.

"Champagne, anyone?"

Nineteen

It took them a while to put out all the candles—mostly because L.J. could not stop laughing.

"You're lucky we didn't go up in blazes," L.J. scolded Cooper as she snuffed the last one.

"We already did," Cooper reminded her huskily. "Or have you forgotten?"

"No, I haven't," L.J. said softly.

But seeing the look smoldering in Cooper's darkened blue gaze, L.J. decided to distract him.

She needed some answers first.

"Whatever possessed you to infest my trailer with all manner of candles, food and flowers?"

Cooper left her side a moment, and came back carrying several romances.

"Mona bought a few for me the Saturday she and Bradford went out together. And I bought a few more."

"Did you read them all?"

"Every last one of them, so help me God," Cooper said with fervor. "Can't you tell?"

"This grand seduction scene—" L.J. waved a hand helplessly, encompassing the whole trailer, while her body began to convulse with laughter again "—it came from a book?"

"Not just one book, sweetheart. Several," Cooper said solemnly. "I decided to incorporate them all—contemporary, historical, futuristic."

L.J. had to sit down. She couldn't take it anymore.

Cooper looked affronted at her lack of appreciation for his effort and creativity.

"After the way I made love to you last week, I was afraid you wouldn't think I was romantic enough. And after you accused me of being no better than Nick—"

L.J. got up, walked over to Cooper and put her hand on his mouth.

"I was wrong. You're not like Nick."

Cooper's expression lightened.

"You're worse."

L.J. giggled, and her mirth died in her throat at Cooper's expression.

"Now, Uncle Coop. Remember, you're getting old and decrepit."

L.J. began backing up, and as Cooper advanced on her, flew to the door and out of it.

She ran around the trailer, feeling Cooper's heavy footsteps behind her.

He caught up to her on a fresh, grassy patch, and brought her down with a modified tackle, managing to break her fall with his own body.

L.J. raised herself on her elbows and looked down on Cooper, the moonlight making his eyes mysterious, dangerous pools.

"You know I love you, don't you?" Cooper asked her, his hands roaming the feminine hollow of her back as she arched her spine away from him.

"Do you, Cooper? Love me? Really love me?" L.J. asked, needing to hear him say it, needing to believe it.

"You must have known it on some level, to have made love with such passionate abandon," Cooper said, and he covered her mouth with his in a whispering touch. This time, instead of an internal inferno, L.J. felt the slow, sweet uncoiling of tension.

"But sometimes love is not enough," L.J. said, licking his lips with the tip of her tongue, and withdrawing it before Cooper could capture it.

Cooper cupped the back of her neck, forcing her to look at him. Really look at him.

"In my case, it is. I'll admit I've been skittish about becoming involved with a woman, letting myself fall in love. I saw the pain my father went through when Mom died. The same happened to an uncle, and my brother, Corbett. But the reluctance never had anything to do with any fear of settling down, of being true to one woman. We Channahons are one-woman men—only, my telling you will never prove it. You'll just have to take a chance on me, and let me show it to you the rest of our lives.''

L.J. held her breath at his declaration, and released it slowly, trying also to release the panic that his words had aroused.

"Are you proposing, Mr. Channahon?''

Cooper could sense, rather than hear, the fear in L.J.'s words.

"I'm in love with you, L.J. And I think you love me, too. But there are no guarantees in life. You'll just have to trust me not to betray you like your father did, like Nick did. I can't promise not to die like your mother did—but I *can* promise you that as long as there is a breath in my body, I will love you. You. And you alone. Forever.''

L.J. dropped quick kisses on Cooper's eyelids, his nose, his chin and then his mouth. But when Cooper would have deepened the contact, she withdrew.

"What about my career, Cooper? I love anthropology and I'll never give it up. After this site, there'll be others. And they may take me away from you, all over the world, for months at a time.''

"Then I'll just have to make sure that you have a ready volunteer, in all of your digs.''

L.J. looked down at him, seeing the clouds that covered the moon play hide-and-seek with his expression, now highlighting it, now darkening it.

"You've got your own job. You can't just pick up and leave—"

"I can, if I become my own boss. I have enough contacts, and I know the business world inside out. I'll just start my own consulting firm. But before I do, I'll make sure a lot of the big companies I represent give donations to a needy project."

"Donations?" L.J. asked as Cooper dug his fingers in her hair and massaged her scalp.

L.J. closed her eyes at the relaxing, divine stroking, and reluctantly opened them again when Cooper said, "Mona has been instrumental in our being together. And she also made me realize that you work far too hard, with too little help. There is no reason why firms should not donate some tax-deductible dollars to a worthy cause."

"Anything in the name of science?"

"Just about," Cooper said, pressing hot kisses along her throat.

Needing to feel his skin on hers, to feel the play of muscle underneath her hands, to have him inside her, L.J. tugged at his buccaneer shirt.

When it wouldn't come undone, she curled her fingers around the collar and pulled. Hard.

The sound of the button being ripped was exciting, and seemed to release their pent-up passion.

Cooper sat up, and tore the shirt from his body.

L.J. threw off her robe, but when Cooper was about to divest her of her nightgown, L.J. asked, "What if someone decides to take a late-night walk?"

"You're right," Cooper said. He lifted the hem of the long gown, just high enough so that it skimmed the top of her thighs.

Ripping the rest of his clothes off, and then her panties, Cooper swallowed one of her breasts into the moistness of his mouth, the wetness puckering the nipple through the thin material.

L.J. straddled Cooper, and squirmed her buttocks over his lower abdomen, watching the play of emotions on his face as he readied himself for her.

She clasped him and squeezed, gently, and his hips bucked off the ground. Moving her hand slowly, up and down the engorged shaft, L.J. saw the powerful chest labor for air, and gently raked a fingernail along the smooth side.

Cooper grabbed her and lifted her, holding her suspended for a hot, eternal instant before he plunged upward. He pulled her onto him with such force that he became deeply embedded, to the point that she felt her internal walls stretching and swelling, trying to accommodate him and his need.

L.J. tried to slow them down, undulating her hips in a leisurely manner. But Cooper rasped his teeth against her nipples, distending them in the mild April night, making them throb with need and causing a corresponding ache to tug at her belly.

Then suddenly he withdrew, leaving her cold and empty, only to surge forward once more. L.J. impaled herself upon him, surrounding him and holding him hostage as her contractions began, all too soon....

Once again, Cooper remained motionless while the spasms shook her, his hands cupping her breasts and kneading them gently.

When she collapsed against him, Cooper thrust upward again, entering and almost withdrawing, building an unbearable rhythm. Then one finger was seeking entry, rubbing against the button that distended under his merciless ministrations.

The friction rose to fever pitch, and their bodies thrashed together, reaching the pinnacle simultaneously.

Cooper, his chest heaving, held her as little tremors shook L.J.'s body, and his hands smoothed over her back and the thighs that were trembling with aftershocks, her knees pulled up and squeezing his ribs spasmodically.

"I think I see spaceships and celestial bodies spinning in the sky," L.J. told him in a voice that seemed to float out of her body.

Cooper chuckled, and L.J. gasped in remembered ecstasy. Her insides were melted, and her nerves raw.

"I think we'd better retreat while we can," Cooper

said. "If we continue out here, we might fall asleep—"

"Heaven forbid," L.J. exclaimed, lowering the hem of her gown.

Cooper gave her the robe, and he picked up the remnants of his buccaneer shirt and discarded slacks.

"I guess it did the trick," Cooper said, touching the cloth that L.J. had so enthusiastically ripped.

L.J. was thankful for the darkness that hid her sudden blush.

She had really acted with total abandon.

But then, she consoled herself, Cooper had not exactly responded like a reclusive monk.

"Do you think any of this is still edible?" Cooper asked a half hour later.

"Who cares?" L.J. answered, pulling him on top of her. "At least we can breathe. The smell is almost all gone."

Cooper chuckled. "Sorry about that. And the Godiva."

"I'll just make sure you keep paying the rest of your life. Now, stop talking and show me how romantic you can be."

Epilogue

Hearing the knock at the door, L.J. hid her head under the pillow.

"If it's the police, tell them to go away."

Cooper got dressed quickly, throwing on an old pair of slacks and shirt that had belonged to Roarke.

"How come Roarke has so many clothes here?"

"Because he brought Bradford over a couple of times as part of his tutorial, and the first time they did, Roarke asked me if he could keep some extra changes here. They slept on the living room floor, in case you're wondering," L.J. told Cooper, looking at him through slitted eyes. "Still jealous? Roarke is a good friend—but *only* a friend. I thought you'd realized that after last night."

"Just wondering," Cooper said, bolting out of the bedroom as another series of knocks threatened to bring down the door.

"Mona, Corbett! What a surprise."

Cooper's words, spoken in a booming voice, woke L.J. up like a bucket of ice water. Leaping off the bed, she slammed the bedroom door closed, and rummaged in the drawers for something to throw on.

The shorts and top might be a bit skimpy considering the weather had once again dipped into the forties this morning in an Illinois spring that was even more changeable than usual, but they were quick to put on.

Swiftly combing through her tousled hair, the snags bringing tears to her eyes, L.J. slowly opened the bedroom door.

Three pairs of eyes, all identical blue, zeroed in on her like lasers.

L.J. swallowed past the nervous lump in her throat, and pasted a smile on her face. She hoped the smile didn't look as sickly as she felt.

"Mona, what a pleasant surprise! What brings you here?"

"The dig, L.J.," Mona said, her shrewd young eyes looking her over. "Uncle Coop took off yesterday without me, so I had to ask Dad here to bring me over."

"I'm Corbett Channahon," Mona's father said, smiling, walking up to L.J. and extending a hand.

"We Channahons are not usually so devoid of manners."

L.J. found she liked Corbett immediately. He was a few years younger than Cooper, taller and slighter of build. But his dark hair and blue eyes were a dead giveaway.

"What, no forgotten textbooks this time, Mona?" Cooper asked his niece.

"Oh, I don't think I'll need to forget anything anymore, Uncle Coop. Not when you so conveniently forgot *me* yesterday."

"Mona, what are you babbling about?" Corbett asked his pride and joy.

"Oh, maybe we'll tell you someday about a plan of mine that worked to perfection," Mona said, smugly.

Corbett turned to L.J., hands splayed helplessly.

"See what I have to deal with? I'm always being kept in the dark."

L.J. and Cooper laughed.

"Well, now that you are here, dear niece, you can get to work and show your father the ropes."

"What ropes?" Corbett asked suspiciously.

"Digging, dear brother. Digging. Anyone showing up at L.J.'s site is an automatic volunteer."

"But I don't know anything about digging or archaeology," Corbett said, alarm fleeting across his handsome face.

"You'll learn, Dad. Nothing to it."

"Is that true, Cooper? Or is this child deceiving me again?"

"Me? Deceive anyone?" Mona asked, her face a study in pure innocence. "That's a nasty accusation."

The three adults looked at Mona and laughed.

"That's not very nice, three grown-ups laughing at a defenseless child," Mona said, a classic study in affront. "There has to be someone who would take my side—"

A crafty look stole over Mona's face.

"Dad, what do you think of UFO's and other unexplained but very probable phenomena?"

Cooper and Mona looked at each other and groaned in unison.

Hooking an arm about Mona's waist, Cooper told his younger brother, "Poor Corbett. You don't know what's in store for you."

Then he bent his dark head and dropped a kiss on L.J.'s lips.

"What do you think, sweetheart? Should we warn him?"

While Corbett looked on in confusion, and Mona in satisfaction, L.J. whispered against Cooper's mouth.

"Let him find out on his own."

* * * * *

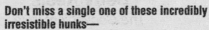

And the Winner Is...
You!

...when you pick up these great titles
from our new promotion at your
favorite retail outlet this June!

Diana Palmer
The Case of the Mesmerizing Boss

Betty Neels
The Convenient Wife

Annette Broadrick
Irresistible

Emma Darcy
A Wedding to Remember

Rachel Lee
Lost Warriors

Marie Ferrarella
Father Goose

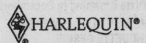 

**This summer, the legend
continues in Jacobsville**

Diana Palmer

A LONG, TALL
TEXAN SUMMER

Three **BRAND-NEW** short stories

This summer, Silhouette brings readers a special
collection for Diana Palmer's LONG, TALL TEXANS
fans. Diana has rounded up three **BRAND-NEW**
stories of love Texas-style, all set in Jacobsville,
Texas. Featuring the men you've grown to love from
this wonderful town, this collection is a must-have
for all fans!

*They grow 'em tall in the saddle in Texas—and
they've got love and marriage on their minds!*

Don't miss this collection of original Long, Tall Texans
stories...available in June at your favorite retail outlet.

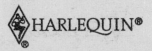

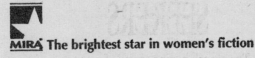